HAP[illegible]
READY [illegible]

Richie pushed his chair back from the breakfast table. "Got to go."

"Don't forget your wallet."

"Where did you say it is?"

"In the drawer," his mother told him. Richie went to the stove and opened the oven door. "I don't see it."

"The *drawer*, Richie, the *drawer*."

"Oh."

He moved to the counter, opened the drawer, and got out his wallet, then returned to the stove, opened the oven, put the wallet in, closed the door, and departed.

Howard and Marian Cunningham looked at each other again.

"Is that our son?" Marian asked.

"On the outside, yes. On the inside . . . I don't know . . ."

"Howard, what has *happened* to him?"

"There are two possibilities," Howard replied. "One, he's inherited his Uncle Frank's absent-mindedness. Two, he's in love."

Also in the *Happy Days* series

No. 1 THE FONZ AND LAZONGA
No. 2 THE BIKE TYCOON
No. 3 DEAR FONZIE
No. 4 FONZIE GOES TO COLLEGE

HAPPY DAYS No. 5
READY TO GO STEADY

William Johnston

UNIVERSAL

A UNIVERSAL BOOK

published by

the Paperback Division of

W. H. ALLEN & Co. Ltd

A Universal Book
Published in 1978
by the Paperback Division of
W. H. Allen & Co. Ltd
A Howard and Wyndham Company
44 Hill Street, London W1X 8LB

Printed in Great Britain by
Hazell Watson & Viney Ltd, Aylesbury, Bucks

ISBN 0 426 18729 6

ONE

"That's hard to believe," Howard Cunningham said, addressing the morning newspaper.

Howard, middle-aged and nicely plump, was seated at the kitchen table, the morning paper opened to an inside page.

"What is, dear?" his wife asked. Marion was at the stove, turning flapjacks. She was sweet-faced and motherly-looking.

"It says here that more people now watch television than listen to radio," Howard told her.

"They said that last year, too."

"I know. But I didn't believe it then, either."

Marion looked disapproving. "Somctimes I think they put things like that in the newspaper just to stir up talk," she said. "I can't think of any other reason. Nobody *has* to know how many people watch television and how many listen to radio."

"It's a sign of the times, Marion. You want to know what's going on, don't you? That's why we get a newspaper."

"I don't want to know everything," she said. "They could have left that out and had room for another recipe on the women's page—something that would do somebody some good. Are you ready?" she asked.

Howard Cunningham put the newspaper aside. "Bring it on."

As Marion was serving breakfast to her husband, their oldest teenage son, Chuck, entered the kitchen and sat down at the table. Chuck was lanky, with a crewcut that just missed being a scalping.

"Good morning, dear," Marion said. "Where are your brother and sister?"

"Joanie's asleep. Richie's talking to himself," Chuck replied.

Marion began piling flapjacks on his plate. "Talking to himself? What is he saying?"

" 'Where did I put that?' "

"He must have lost something. Oh—I know," Marion said. "His wallet. I found it on the front porch steps this morning when I went out to get the paper."

"He's had that billfold one day," Howard said. "How many times has he lost it?"

"Three that I know of," Marion replied, going back to the stove. "But don't say anything about it, Howard. He has a lot on his mind, starting on that job today." She went to the counter and opened a drawer and got out the wallet. "It's a big moment for him. He's never had a summer job before."

"I know, Marion. I'm his father, I live here—remember?"

She returned to the table and placed the wallet on her second son's plate. "There—he'll see it when he comes down. We won't say a word about him losing it."

"Uh-huh. He'll think it dropped out of his pocket while he was doing handsprings on the kitchen table."

"I just don't want him to go to his first day on the job feeling unsure of himself," Marion said, going back to the stove. "It's important to have confidence."

"It's a job in a warehouse. He'll be loading and unloading. How much confidence does that take?"

"It's the idea," Marion said. "Attitude is—" At the sound of whistling coming from the hallway, she interrupted herself. "Here he comes!"

Richie Cunningham breezed into the kitchen. " 'Morning!" he said, beaming. "I smelled flapjacks all the way upstairs."

"Sit down, dear," his mother said.

Richie pulled out a chair and settled at the table and picked up the syrup pitcher and began pouring syrup on his wallet. "Boy, I could eat a horse," he said.

"What are you telling us, Richie?" his father asked. "That that billfold is made out of horsehide?"

Richie suddenly saw what he was doing. "Oh, boy!" He put the pitcher down and snatched up the wallet and ran to the sink with it and began rinsing the syrup from it. "Lucky I haven't got my pay in here," he said. "The college probably wouldn't take sticky money."

Howard and Marion Cunningham looked at each other. Howard shrugged, indicating that he didn't know what his son was talking about either.

"What college, dear?' Marion asked.

"I'm not sure yet," Richie answered, beginning to dry the wallet. "What I meant was, when I *do* start to college. That's what I'm going to do with the money I make this summer, save it up for college." He returned to the table, stuffing the wallet into his back pocket "That's the reason for getting the job Didn't I tell you?"

"No, you didn't," his father said. "But, Richie, that's very commendable."

"It certainly is, dear," his mother said, stacking flapjacks on his plate. "I'm proud of you."

"Well, I'm not a kid anymore," Richie said. "I've got to start thinking ahead."

"Like looking where you're pouring your syrup?" Howard Cunningham said.

Chuck rose. "Got to go," he announced.

"Where, dear?"

"Beach. Some of the guys," Chuck replied, departing.

"He'll be sorry one of these days," Richie said, when Chuck had gone. "Remember the ant and the grasshopper?" he said solemnly to his father.

"They sound familiar," Howard Cunningham replied. "Are they the guys Chuck is going to the beach with?"

"No, you remember. The ant was putting away nuts for the winter and the grasshopper was hopping around—"

"I think it's squirrels who put away nuts for the winter, Richie."

"Well, whatever. When winter came, the ant was prepared, but the grasshopper was out in the cold. That's the way it is," he said. "Most of my friends are like that, too. Of all the guys I know, I'm the only one with a summer job."

"Jobs are scarce this summer, I understand," his father said. "I read that in the paper."

"That paper," Marion said disdainfully.

"Marion, it's not the newspaper's fault."

"I don't know," Richie said. "I got a job, didn't I? I'm not saying anything about anybody, but if they tried a little harder . . ." He frowned thoughtfully. "I guess some guys just mature faster than others," he said.

"Don't get your beard in your syrup," his father said.

Richie looked at him puzzledly. "What beard?"

"Oh, sorry . . . there for a second, I saw you with a long white beard. Must have been my imagination."

"Howard, don't make fun," Marion said. "I think it's wonderful that Richie is showing so much responsibility."

"That's okay, Mom," Richie said. He addressed his father again. "What's in the paper this morning?"

"More people watch television than listen to radio."

Richie frowned again. "Mmmmmm . . . this would be a good time to buy television stocks," he said. "Get in on the ground floor."

His mother suddenly looked worried. "Now, dear, don't be too mature," she said. "Save for college first. One thing at a time."

"Don't worry, Mom," Richie replied, getting up. "I'm not in that league—yet. Well, got to be running," he said, going toward the exit. Then, at the door, he halted. "Mom, have you seen my yo-yo?"

She went to the counter and opened the drawer again. "This one?" she asked, holding up a yellow yo-yo.

"That's it," Richie said, taking it from her. He hesitated. "Something to do on the way to work," he explained to his father.

"I'm glad to see that," Howard Cunningham said. "I'm very big in yo-yo stocks, you know."

Richie grinned sheepishly. "See you."

Spinning the yo-yo, Richie left the house and walked leisurely toward the bus stop. When he was halfway up the block, he saw the moving van parked in front of the second house from the corner. Men were unloading furnitiure and carrying it up the walk. Seeing a girl his age and a boy, younger, standing on the porch, Richie reeled in the yo-yo. The girl was uncommonly attractive.

Nearing the truck, Richie halted and watched the men unload a sofa. When they started toward the house with it, he followed them with his eyes—and then managed to look surprised when he saw that the girl and boy were observing him. He smiled amiably. The girl smiled back. The boy just stared.

"Moving in?" Richie called to them.

"Yes," the girl replied. "Do you live around here?"

"Couple houses back," Richie answered. He walked toward the porch. "Where you from?"

"Springfield."

"Oh. I'm Richie Cunningham."

"I'm Emma Watt," the girl told him. She indicated the boy, who appeared to be nine or ten. "This is my brother Bobs."

"Hi," Richie said. "I was just on my way to work and I saw the moving van."

"It just got here," Emma said. "Where do you work?"

"Oh . . . Mid-State Distributors. It's a food supply place. You know, groceries. We supply all the food stores around here in this area. Sort of a warehouse, I guess you might say."

"Oh. That's nice."

"It's incorporated," Richie said.

"Gee."

"I could have been incorporated," Bobs Watt said.

Richie peered at him.

"I was in the junk business in Springfield," the boy told him. "I had to sell out."

Richie continued to stare at him.

"He's advanced for his age," Emma told Richie. "What do you do at— What's the name of it?"

"Mid-State. I don't know what I do yet exactly. This is my first day. A little of this and a little of that probably. You know how it is. It's a summer job. I'm saving up to go to college."

Emma brightened. "That's wonderful. I might go to college, too. If I keep my grades up, my father says."

"These days, if you want to be anybody, you almost have to go to college," Richie said.

"I had a college kid working for me when I was in the junk business," Bobs said.

Richie stared at him again.

"It was only in the summer," Emma explained. "Like you have a summer job—it wasn't full-time."

"When I get my operation going again, maybe I'll put you on," Bobs told Richie.

Richie blinked.

"You're lucky, having something to do," Emma told Richie. "My whole summer is really going to be blah, I guess. I don't know anybody, you know. I'll just have to sit around twiddling my thumbs, I suppose."

"Nah, you'll get acquainted. It's easy."

"For a boy, it is. But not for a girl. I can't just go up to people and introduce myself."

"Hey, listen, I could take you around," Richie said.

"I wouldn't want to put you out."

"No, it's nothing. What are you doing tonight? I'll show you the town."

"Are you *sure* you wouldn't mind?"

"Heck, no. I didn't have anything to do, anyway. Usually, I just sit around and read the paper and keep up on stocks and things like that."

"What're you in?" Bobs asked him.

"Huh?"

"What stocks?"

"Oh, well, none, not exactly," Richie replied. "I just like to think ahead." He addressed Emma again. "Pick you up around eight?"

"That would be just wonderful."

Richie backed away. "Okay . . . see you then. . . ."

"Nice meeting you."

"See me about those stocks before you get your feet wet," Bobs said.

"Yeah . . . will do. . . ."

The Mid-state warehouse was located near the edge of town. It was a large, two-story brick building, with loading docks, where the food manufacturers' trucks delivered their products, and where the Mid-State trucks loaded up the products to distribute to the grocery stores Mid-State serviced.

Arriving, Richie reported to the supervisor, Edgar Starch, whose small office was near the loading docks. Starch was the man who had hired him the day before. He was middle-aged and chunky and balding and had a gruff but not unpleasant manner. His eyes, behind rimless spectacles, had a somewhat distracted look, giving him the appearance of having forgotten something important and knowing that he would never remember what it was.

"Here I am," Richie said, confronting Starch at his desk.

The supervisor looked up. "What?"

"Here I am—sir."

"Fine. What for?"

"I'm ready to go to work."

An invisible light bulb flashed on over Starch's head. "Oh, right, sure," he said. "You're the new kid. I forgot there for a minute." He nodded toward the door. "Go find Joe Ferguson," he told Richie. "He'll tell you what to do."

"Yes, sir." Richie moved toward the door, then paused. "Do you have any idea where he is?" he asked.

"Goofing off, if I know Ferguson," Starch said. "Just yell around for him, you'll find him."

Richie left the office. At one of the docks, two boys his own age were unloading cartons of canned sweet peas from a truck. He asked them if they knew where he could find Joe Ferguson.

"Listen for snoring and follow that," one of the boys told him.

"Look under all the empty boxes," the other boy said.

Richie moved on, looking down the rows between the towering stacks of food cartons. He got glimpses of other boys pushing hand trucks loaded with boxes and crates. When he reached the final row, he saw a young man at the far end. He was tall and gangly and looked to be about twenty, and he was pulling an enormous cardboard carton from a pile Richie walked toward him.

Having placed the carton in the aisle, the young man was opening the top flaps. Approaching, Richie watched him curiously. The young man began climbing the nearby stack of boxes. He reached a height that was at least six feet off the floor, then looked down into the enormous carton. Richie got the impression that he intended to jump down into it.

"Joe Ferguson?" Richie called out.

The young man, surprised, looked down at him. "Who're you?"

"Richie Cunningham. Mr. Starch told me to see you."

"What about?" Joe Ferguson asked suspiciously.

"He told me you'd tell me what to do. I'm starting work."

Ferguson grinned. It was a grin like a slice of watermelon. "I thought old Starch sent you around to spy on me," he said. "That guy's a slave-driver. But, that's okay, just play it cozy," he said. "I'll take care of you. Just take your cues from Joe Ferguson and everything'll be copacetic." He began climbing down. "Richie? That your moniker?"

Richie nodded.

"I was about to make a box inspection," Joe Ferguson told him. "We don't want any cheap goods coming in here. So, every once in a while, you know, I make a spot check. I get inside a box and check it out. You can't tell from the outside."

Richie nodded again.

"Come on," Joe said, heading up the aisle. "You married?" he asked, as Richie fell in beside him.

"No, I'm still in school. I'm just here for the summer."

"Never make plans," Joe said. "Who knows? Maybe you'll like it here. Maybe you'll stay. You ought to get married, Richie. It's the greatest. I been married two months now. I guarantee—it's a whirl."

"I'm kind of young yet," Richie said.

"You'll never get any younger."

"Huh?"

"The only thing you can get, I mean, is older—right? Did you ever think about it, Richie? You know—you're dying. Right now, you're dying. It starts the day you're born. Right away, you start dying. Am I right?"

"If you look at it that way, I guess," Richie conceded.

"You're a dying man, Richie," Joe said. "So, think about it, what do you want to do with the time you've got left? Waste it in school?" They reached the end of the aisle and walked toward the loading docks. "I could've stayed in school. It was a breeze. But, one day, I woke up. I asked myself: Joe, what'll it get you?"

"I don't think my dad would like it if I quit."

"You have to grab the bull by the horns," Joe told him. "Look at me. I've got it made. A hot little wife—you ought to meet my wife, Millie. A real looker. I've got this job—and it's like money in the bank." He winked. "Me and the Big Boss, we're side by side, know what I mean?"

"Mr. Starch?"

"Nah, not Starch. He's small potatoes. I'm talking about the *Big Boss*—Charles M. Coogan himself. I call him Charlie. My wife's mother is his sister. That makes him her uncle. She's his niece. You know what that makes me, don't you?"

"Uhhhh . . ."

"Johnny-on-the spot," Joe told him. "The world is my oyster. You ought to meet my wife, Millie. Some stuff." They were passing the dock where the boys were unloading. "See those guys," he said. "They're school boys, too, just like you. But ask yourself this: what'll it get them? By the time they get out of school, I'll have the experience, see? I'll probably be running this whole outfit. They'll come around to me and I'll say to them: okay, boys, what did you learn in school about the distribution business? Nothing, they'll tell me. Sorry, boys, I'll say, but I can't use you. Your heads are full of facts and figures, but you don't know nothing. Know what I mean?"

"Yeah, only—"

"Stick with me, Richie. When I move up, you know, I'll need somebody to take my place. It could be you."

They reached the final tier of cartons.

"See these six stacks?" Joe Ferguson said.

Richie nodded.

"What does it say on them?"

"Garden Sweet succotash."

"Some dumb bunny piled the succotash here and it's supposed to be two aisles back," Joe said. "We got to move it. Get yourself a truck."

Richie went looking for a hand truck and found one a short distance away. When he returned, Joe Ferguson had got down a carton of succotash and was seated on it.

"Load it up," Joe said.

Richie began piling the cartons on the truck.

"You ought to meet my wife, Millie," Joe said, still sitting. "There's a doll We've got an apartment. Ever live in an apartment?"

"Nope."

"It's the only way to live. You don't have to worry about it, you know. It's not yours. With a house, you have to think about keeping it up. But with an apartment, it's the landlord's tough luck. Know what I mean?"

"Sort of," Richie replied. He was beginning to sweat.

"Take your shirt off," Joe suggested.

"I guess I will."

"I go around the apartment with no shirt on," Joe said. "That's what you can do when you're married. You want to know something? Sometimes I go around with a lot less than no shirt on." He made clucking sounds. "Think about that for a while! Gets your steam up, eh?"

Richie leaned against a stack of cartons, panting. "I didn't know these things were so heavy," he said.

"You don't have to tell me—I'm the one who stacked them up there," Joe said.

Richie remembered that Joe Ferguson had told him that the cartons had been piled in the wrong place by some dumb bunny.

"You ought to see what goes on in that apartment sometimes," Joe said. "Ever been to a burleyque?"

Richie shook his head.

"It's better than the burleyque sometimes," Joe told him. "That's the way it is when you're married, you know. No holds barred."

"Not around my house," Richie said.

"Who's married at your house?"

"My parents."

"Oh, yeah, well, that's different. That's the way old-fashioned people are," Joe said. "But, with modern guys and gals, it's one big party."

Richie began piling cartons onto the truck again.

"That's the way it is with Millie and me, anyway," Joe went on. "Richie, let me tell you something. Life is for the living. Enjoy it now. Because, after you're dead, the kicks are over. I know what you're thinking—you're thinking that's just common sense. But how many people live up to it? Ask yourself that."

"Do you think I've got too many on here?" Richie said, looking at the stack of cartons on the truck.

"Way too many," Joe replied. "You try to move that truck and those boxes'll be all over the place."

Richie began reducing the load.

"Ninety-nine per cent of the people spend their whole lives saving up for a rainy day," Joe told him. "And, by the time it rains, they're six foot under. Get what I mean?"

Richie grunted.

"Millie and me, we're modern. I'll tell you how modern we are—Millie works. She's got a job. She's a secretary. That's the modern girl for you, Richie. Anything we want, we get it. We can afford it. You know what I could do right now? I could take out a five-dollar bill, Richie, and I could set fire to it. No kidding. Money to burn." He winked again. "How'd you like to be able to live that way?"

"Okay."

"But that's not the best part."

"What is?"

"Do you know what risque is?" Joe asked.

"Sexy?"

"Right. And that's the word that describes me and Millie. We risque all over the house. Anytime we want to. You can do that when you're married."

Richie turned away, feeling a warmth in his face. "I guess I can move this stuff now," he said. "Where did you say it goes?"

"Two aisles back," Joe replied, rising. "I'll go with you and show you."

Richie got behind the cart and pushed. It barely budged.

"Get some back into it there," Joe said.

Grunting, Richie put all his strength into the push. The truck began rolling. Joe walked on ahead, leading the way.

"I'll take you up to the apartment someday and you can meet Millie," Joe said. "But when you shake hands, watch it—she's hot stuff."

"How much farther?" Richie asked, straining.

"Right here."

Richie stopped pushing. But it was a second before he could straighten up. His muscles seemed permanently cramped.

"This is succotash," Joe told him, indicating a section. "Pile it here. Don't go too far, though. Don't run into tomatoes."

"Don't run into tomatoes," Richie said numbly, nodding.

"See you," Joe told him, strolling off. "Got to go to that box check."

TWO

When Richie got off the bus that afternoon, returning from work, his arms hung at his sides like two long, limp sausages. He had been lifting, pushing and pulling crates and cartons and boxes the entire day, save for the brief break for lunch. He felt as if every bone and muscle in his body had been rendered to pulp. He managed to keep his head up only because he knew that if it dropped off he would be unable to bend over and pick it up.

Richie had gone only a few steps when he heard someone calling to him. He halted, sighed, then, with effort, turned around. The bus was still standing at the curb. The door was open and a sweet-faced little old lady was standing on the step. She was holding something out toward Richie. Walking back to the bus, he recognized the object—it was his wallet.

"You left your billfold on the seat," the little old lady told him.

"Gee, thanks," he said, retrieving the wallet. "A lot of people wouldn't go to that trouble."

"Think nothing of it," she said. "It only has a buck in it."

The little old lady retreated, the door closed and the bus rolled on.

Shaking his head in dismay, Richie headed toward home once more.

Plodding on, he soon reached the Watt house, where that morning he had met Emma and her younger brother Bobs. The moving in had been completed. At the moment, there was not a Watt in sight. Thinking about Emma, Richie perked up a bit. She was a real looker. She wouldn't have any trouble getting acquainted—especially with the boys—once the ice was broken. Too bad. It would be nice to have a looker like Emma all to himself for the whole summer.

Approaching his home, Richie saw two of his friends, Potsie and Ralph, walking toward him. He immediately straightened, wanting to conceal his weariness. Neither Potsie nor Ralph had summer jobs. Richie put on a wide grin as they drew closer, then, as if unable to contain an excess of energy, he pantomimed a few dribbles with a basketball and faked a hook shot at an imaginary basket.

"Didn't you go to that job today?" Potsie asked.

"Sure," Richie replied.

"What is it, a snap?" Ralph asked.

"No, it's heavy work," Richie said. "But if you're in shape, it's nothing. It's good for you. By fall, I'll be all muscle."

"You're really lucky, getting that job," Potsie said. "The guys were talking about it today. By the end of summer, you'll be loaded. What're you going to do with all that money?"

"Who knows? There's a lot of things."

"I'd get a car," Ralph said.

"What'd you guys do today?" Richie asked.

We went out to the junction and saw Fonzie off," Potsie told him. "He's hitching west this summer."

"Yeah, and then we went out to the lake," Ralph said.

"Who was out there?"

"Everybody," Potsie said. "You're about the only lucky one in the crowd. Nobody else can find a job."

"It's going to be like that all summer," Ralph said. "Just hanging around and horsing around with the girls. Really boring."

"I hear somebody moved in on your block," Potsie said to Richie. "Anybody interesting?"

"What would anybody interesting be doing in this town?" he replied.

"Yeah," Potsie agreed.

"It's so boring," Ralph said, "we talked today about going out camping maybe." He smiled wickedly. "If we can get some of the girls to go."

"Fat chance," Potsie said. "But it's worth a try."

"Are you going to be around tonight?" Ralph asked Richie.

"I don't think so," he answered. "I'll probably read the newspaper."

"All night?" Potsy said.

"There's a lot in the newspaper besides 'Steve Canyon,'" Richie said. "Some of that stuff is really interesting. Do you know that more people watch television these days than listen to radio?"

"Yeah," Potsie replied. "My father read that to my mother this morning."

"That's hard to believe," Ralph said.

"But, even if you know it, what can you do with it?" Potsie said.

"Get in on the ground floor in television," Richie said. "How do you think guys get rich? They read the paper. That's something I might do with the money I make—play the market."

"Hey!" Potsie said, impressed.

"And we'll just be hanging around," Ralph said glumly. "You're really lucky, Richie, getting that job. By the end of summer, you're going to have everything."

"If I don't save it and use it to go to college," Richie said. "That's an investment, too."

"How?" Ralph asked.

"It's an investment in yourself, in your future," Richie told him.

"What'd you do, read that in the paper?" Ralph asked.

"I don't know. I heard it someplace, I think." He nodded toward the house. "I got to go, guys."

"See you," Potsie said.

"If you get finished with the paper and decide to come out tonight, you know where we'll be—hanging around," Ralph said.

"Some other night," Richie said.

"Okay."

Richie entered the house. Immediately, his muscles became flab again. He sagged.

"Richie—is that you?" his mother called from the kitchen.

"Yeah, Mom."

"How was your day, dear?"

Richie searched his mind for the right word. It wasn't there. "Enriching," he called back.

"What?"

"Stimulating," Richie replied, dragging himself toward the stairs.

"That's nice."

A few minutes later, he reached his room and collapsed across the bed. As his muscles relaxed and the aches subsided, he was struck by an encouraging thought: the best was yet to come; there was no possible way that, physically, he could feel any worse.

Richie arrived at the Watt house at eight. His knock was answered by Mrs. Watt, a short, plump woman, with a bubbly manner. She was carrying a large lamp. When Richie introduced himself and explained his presence, she went to the bottom of the stairs and called up to Emma, announcing his arrival. Emma called back, saying that she would be down in a minute.

"That just gives us time," Mrs. Watt said to Richie. "Would you do me a favor, dear?" she said, motioning him into the living room. "I'm trying to place this lamp."

The living room was yet to be arranged. The chairs and sofa were at odd angles. The rug was still rolled up. The tables were piled with unopened boxes.

Mrs. Watt stood Richie in a corner and handed him the lamp, then backed away.

"A little higher, dear," she said. "Be a tall table."

Richie raised the lamp.

A tall, thin, graying man entered the room and stood beside Mrs. Watt. Together, they resembled somewhat a bowling ball and a tenpin.

"What do you think?" Mrs. Watt asked the man.

"I have to see it with the chair," he replied.

Mrs. Watt introduced Richie to the man. He was Mr. Watt. Then Mr. Watt moved a chair, placing it beside Richie. That done, he returned to his wife's side.

"I don't know," he said. "I like it and I don't."

"Up, up, dear—hold the lamp up," Mrs. Watt said to Richie.

His arm was aching.

Bobs, the son, came into the room. "It ought to be over by the window," he said.

"I think you're right, dear," his mother said.

She took Richie by the hand and led him to the window, then went back to stand with her husband and son.

"Better . . . but just not . . . I don't know . . . ," Mrs. Watt said.

"You don't want that tall table there," her husband said.

"Yes, maybe that's it. Lower the lamp, dear," she said to Richie.

Grateful, he brought his arm down.

"No, darling, you're not being a table," she told him. "Hold the lamp up, but bend your knees—sort of squat."

Richie obeyed.

"Yes, now *that*'s a table," she said approvingly.

Emma arrived. "Hi," she said to Richie, smiling admiringly.

"I don't know if I can talk," he answered. "I'm a table."

"Mother, Richie didn't come over to be a table," Emma said to Mrs. Watt.

"Darling, you were upstairs, you weren't using him."

"Well, are you finished with him now?"

Mrs. Watt sighed. "Oh, I suppose so Harold," she said to her husband, "you hold the lamp"

"I'm the tall table," he said. "Better let Bobs do it"

Mrs. Watt took the lamp from Richie. "No," she said, "he's too short for the short table."

Richie eased by her and he and Emma moved toward the entryway.

"Stand him on a box," Mr. Watt suggested.

"Well . . . if we can find a short box. . . ."

Richie and Emma reached the door, then slipped out of the house.

"I'm sorry," Emma said, as she and Richie walked up the street.

"That's okay," he said. "Sometimes I'm the table at home, too, when my mother is trying to find a place to put a lamp."

Emma laughed and they walked along in silence for a few moments.

"I almost once went to a college," Emma said.

"Huh?"

"You told me this morning that you're saving up to go to college. I said I almost once went to college. They were having the homecoming weekend and a boy invited me. He was a freshman. But my mother and father wouldn't let me go."

"Why not?"

"It was for the whole weekend. They're old-fashioned."

"They have chaperones or something, don't they?"

She nodded. "But my father said I could only go if the chaperone was handcuffed to me. He doesn't think chaperones are much good when it comes to college." She looked up at him. "Where are we going?"

"Want to see the park?"

"Sure."

When they reached the park, they walked along the edge of the small lagoon, then stopped at the statue of the Civil War general on horseback.

"Which general is he?" Emma asked.

"Gee, I don't know." Richie examined the base, looking for an inscription. "It doesn't say," he reported. "Maybe it did, but it's worn off. This statue's been here a long time. My father told me once it was here when he was my age. And that was when I was just a kid."

"It can't be General Grant—he doesn't have a cigar," Emma said.

"It must be Stonewall Pershing."

"I think it is."

As they walked on, Emma slipped her hand into Richie's.

"Want to see the filtration plant?" Richie asked.

"What's that?"

"That's where they purify the water."

"All right."

"It's kind of a long walk," Richie said, having second thoughts.

"I don't care."

So they set out toward the edge of town. On the way, Richie pointed out the library, which was closed.

"Is your whole family cultured?" Emma asked.

Richie considered for a second. "In what way?" he asked.

"You know, interested in statues and libraries."

"Well, my mother gets books out of the library a

lot," he confessed. "And my father remembers that statue. But we don't go overboard."

"You're more balanced," she said.

"Yeah, more balanced. My brother's a basketball nut."

"You're probably well-rounded," she said.

"I guess you could say that."

The rest of the way to the filtration plant, they talked about the high school. Richie told Emma which teachers were easy and which were tough. He advised her to try to avoid getting Mrs. McCormack for World History because she made her students memorize dates.

By the time they reached their destination, Richie's muscles were aching again. They sat down on the hill above the filtration plant and watched the turning of the huge vertical wheel as it kept the sediment in the town's water supply on the move.

"It's beautiful," Emma said dreamily.

"The moonlight helps," Richie said. "It's not much in the daylight."

"The way it just keeps turning, it's just like life, isn't it?" Emma said.

"How do you mean?"

"Well, the world is billions of years old, you know. It's like a wheel, turning and turning, never stopping."

"The filtration plant stopped once," Richie told her. "We couldn't turn on the faucets for a whole day."

"What'd you do for something to drink?"

"Cokes."

"Oh." She slipped her hand into his again. "Isn't that just like humankind," she said. "We always find a way to survive. I had a biology teacher who said that once. It's really beautiful if you think about it."

"People started hoarding Cokes," Richie said. "By noon, you couldn't buy any. Except from one guy. He had crates of them and he was selling them for a dollar a bottle."

"He sounds like Bobs," she said.

"Then they turned the water on again." He faced her. "I had a sip of one of those dollar Cokes," he said.

"You've really had a lot of experience, haven't you?"

Richie looked toward the filtration plant again. "Some guys just mature faster than others," he said.

They left the hill a short while later and walked slowly—because Richie was still feeling the pain of the day's hard labor—back toward town. Returning by a different route, they passed within a block of Arnold's drive-in where Richie's friends hung out. The drive-in was brightly lighted and cars were pulling in and backing out and the babble of the patrons could be heard faintly from that distance.

"Is that where everybody goes?" Emma asked.

"A lot do," he replied. "A lot of the guys hang out there. It's okay, if that's all you want to do—hang out."

Emma seemed to be looking longingly in the direction of the drive-in.

"They're just kids," Richie told her. He knew what would happen if he took her to the drive-in and introduced her to his friends. He would lose her. His friends had their days free. Emma would begin spending her days at the beach with them. Before long, he would be just another face in the crowd. "Not one of them is thinking ahead—about college," he said.

Reluctantly, Emma gave him her full attention again.

When they reached the Watt house, the lights were

still on. Richie and Emma stopped on the porch. Mrs. Watt's voice could be heard, as she directed Mr. Watt and Bobs in the arranging of the furniture.

"Want to come in?" Emma asked.

"I guess not." He was in no condition to be drafted into service as a furniture mover.

"Well . . . ," Emma said.

"There's a lot of the town yet we didn't see," Richie said.

"It's getting kind of late."

"No, I mean maybe some other time."

"I'd like that."

"Even tomorrow night maybe."

"That'd be fun," she said.

"Well . . . ," Richie said.

"It was nice."

He nodded.

"Well . . ."

"I'll see you tomorrow night," Richie said. He turned away.

" Richie. . . ."

"Yeah?" he said, halting and facing her again.

Then it happened. She launched herself at him. Her arms locked around his neck. She pulled his head down and mashed her mouth against his. Overwhelmed, Richie could do nothing but stand and marvel. The kiss was bruising and passionate—an adult kiss. A picture of Rita Hayworth and a leading man locked in just such an embrace flashed briefly through his mind. This was the real thing!

Just as Richie was recovering from the shock and about to begin participating in the kiss, Emma suddenly broke free. She stood looking into his eyes for a second—questioningly, perhaps. Then, before he could move or speak, she turned away and opened the door and disappeared into the house. Still mildly stunned, Richie stared fascinatedly at the space that she had so recently occupied. He had the feeling of having been treated to a small bite of something especially tasty, then having had it snatched away.

From inside came Mrs. Watt's voice. "Oh, here you are, darling." Evidently she was addressing Emma. "Be a floor lamp, will you, please, dear, and stand in that corner over there. Your father is tired of lugging it around."

The sound cracked, although it did not completely shatter, Richie's spell. He fled.

Richie's father was in the living room, reading the evening paper, when Richie entered the house.

"Hello," Howard Cunningham said. "How are all the hamburgers at the drive-in?"

"I didn't go there," Richie replied.

His father lowered the paper. "What happened? Did it burn down?"

"No. We've got a new family on the block. They've got a daughter. I sort of took her on a tour, showed her the sights."

"The sights?" Howard said. "I didn't know we had any."

"You know, that statue in the park, and the filtration plant and the library, like that," Richie said. "All the cultural spots."

His father stared at him.

"I'll probably show her the rest of the town tomorrow night," Richie said. "I sort of promised."

"What's left?"

Richie thought for a moment. "There's the bus station." He sat down. "What's in the paper?" he said.

"The same old thing, just a lot of news."

"How's television?"

"Moronic, the last time I looked," Howard Cunningham replied.

"No, I mean the television business. Any news about that?"

"If there is, I haven't come to it yet. I just finished with 'Steve Canyon.' " He studied Richie closely. "Are you feeling all right?" he asked. "You look a little . . . a little dazed. . . ."

"I'm fine," Richie assured him.

"Didn't walk into a telephone pole or anything?"

"Huh-uh."

"You didn't drop anything on your head at work. . . ."

"No, honest."

"All right." Howard Cunningham raised the paper. "There is a story in here that might interest you," he said. "It's on the minimum wage. A congressman wants to raise it. You do get the minimum wage, I suppose."

"I don't know. They didn't tell me."

"If they didn't tell you, then, believe me, you get the minimum wage," Howard said. "Here, I'll read you the story . . . ."

Richie listened for a few seconds. Then his attention wandered. He saw Rita Hayworth again. Now, though, he knew who her leading man was. It was Richie himself who was making passionate love to the screen goddess. And, perhaps not so surprisingly, Rita Hayworth had come to resemble Emma Watt somewhat.

The kiss was certainly Emma's. She was hurting his mouth.

"... Of course, I don't know exactly how much that would mean to you in dollars and cents," Richie's father said.

"Huh?"

"I said I don't know how much of a raise you would get."

"For what?"

"Richie, weren't you listening?"

"Oh . . . yeah. . . ." He touched his fingers to his mouth. "I'm not bleeding, am I?"

"You *did* walk into a telephone pole!" his father said.

"Is it really bleeding?"

"No. Why would your mouth be bleeding?"

"I thought I bit my lip."

"Oh. Richie, don't you think you ought to go to bed? You still have that dazed look. I think you worked too hard today."

"I do kind of ache," Richie admitted.

He got up, then stood, smiling wistfully, staring vacantly.

"Richie. . . ."

"Huh?"

"If you're waiting for your room to come downstairs and get you and take you up, I don't think it'll happen," Howard Cunningham said.

Richie started toward the stairs.

"Oh, I forgot . . . who're the new neighbors?" his father asked.

"Watt."

"I said 'who are the new neighbors?' "

Richie halted. "I just told you."

"What?"

"Right."

"Richie, am I Abbot and you're Costello, or is it the other way around?"

"That's their name—Watt. W-a-t-t. He's Mr. Watt and she's Mrs. Watt."

"And the daughter?"

Richie smiled softly. "Emma," he said.

"Any others?"

"Bobs. He's a junk dealer."

"Oh. How old is he?"

"Nine . . . ten. . . ."

"A ten-year-old junk dealer? I'll have to go down and meet them."

Richie started up the stairs, then paused. "I'd wait a few days, if I were you, Dad," he said. "Mrs. Watt might turn you into a lamp." Then he went on up.

Howard Cunningham made a face. "Turn me into a lamp, eh? Well, at least that explains his dazed look. We've got a family of witches in the neighborhood. They put the whammy on him."

THREE

A series of loud thumps came from the front of the house.

At the kitchen table, Howard Cunningham raised his eyes from the morning newspaper and looked at his wife, who had turned from the stove to look at him.

"Do you think the living room fell in?" Howard said. "Or was that just Richie coming down the stairs?"

"I hope it was the living room," she said. "If it was Richie, I think he *fell* down the stairs."

Richie appeared. He was carrying one shoe.

"Was that you?" his father asked him.

Richie pulled out a chair, "Was what me?"

"The living room falling in."

"Oh," he said, sitting down. "Yeah, that was me. I fell down the stairs. I was trying to put on my shoe while I was coming down, and I sort of lost my balance."

"You're not hurt, are you?" his mother asked.

"I don't know . . . I think I did something to my left foot," Richie replied. "It feels funny."

Howard Cunningham leaned over, peering at his son's left foot. "I wonder if it's because you're wearing your right shoe on it?" he said.

Richie brightened. "Hey—you're right!"

"How do you want your eggs, dear?" his mother asked.

"Medium," Richie answered, removing the right shoe from the left foot.

Howard and Marion Cunningham exchanged looks, then they both focused on Richie again.

"Medium eggs?" Marion said. "What exactly is that?"

"Oh, did you say eggs?" Richie responded. "I thought you said oatmeal. Scrambled eggs, I gucss."

The parents looked at each other again.

"If you want to ask him what medium oatmeal is, go ahead, but don't expect me to do it," Howard said to Marion. "I don't want to know."

Marion turned back to the stove and began preparing her son's breakfast. "Incidentally, dear, if you're looking for your wallet," she said to Richie, "it's in the drawer. I found it in the bathroom wastebasket when I was emptying it."

Richie reached into his back pocket and pulled out a torn wrapper from a bar of soap. "I guess I got a little mixed up," he said. "I was washing up and dressing at the same time last night and I opened a new bar of soap and I guess I threw my billfold away and. . . ." He shrugged.

"Richie, speaking of your billfold," his father said. "You've had that job over two weeks now. I hope you're not carrying all that money around with you."

Richie shook his head. "I keep it in my drawer." He frowned. "Or is it under the mattress?" Then he brightened again. "No, it's not under the mattress. I put it there first, but it hung down through the springs.

So I put it in the drawer—" The frown returned. "—I think."

"Why don't you put it in the bank?" Howard Cunningham suggested.

"What if somebody robs the bank?"

"What if you're cleaning up your room someday and you throw out your dresser drawer instead of the trash?" his father countered.

Richie looked at him perplexedly. "Why would I do that?"

"Why would you throw out your billfold and keep a soap wrapper?"

"Maybe I better put it in the bank," Richie conceded.

His mother placed a plate of scrambled eggs in front of him. "Eat. You don't want to miss your bus."

"What are you and Emma doing these days?" Richie's father asked him, as Richie began on the breakfast. "I'm sure you've run out of 'sights' by now."

"We do a lot of window shopping," Richie said.

"Well, don't buy any. We have all the windows we need."

"Window shopping for what, dear?" Marion Cunningham asked her son.

"Nothing. We look at furniture a lot."

Marion winced.

"For any particular reason?" Richie's father asked him.

"Emma just likes to look at furniture," he replied. "It must be a hobby. Her mother likes to move furniture a lot—she probably caught it from her."

"I know," Howard said. "When I went down to introduce myself, she had me pushing the sofa around."

"She made me get down on my hands and knees in the entryway," Marion said.

Howard looked at her questioningly.

"A telephone table," Marion explained.

Richie pushed back his chair, rising. "Got to go."

"Don't forget your wallet."

"Where did you say it is?"

"In the drawer," his mother told him.

Richie went to the stove and opened the oven door. "I don't see it."

"The *drawer,* Richie, the *drawer."*

"Oh."

He moved on to the counter, opened the drawer, and got out his wallet, then returned to the stove, opened the oven, put the wallet in, closed the door, and departed.

Howard and Marion Cunningham looked at each other again.

"Is that our son?" Marion asked.

"On the outside, yes. On the inside . . . I don't know. . . ."

"Howard, what has *happened* to him?"

"There are two possibilities," Howard replied. "One, he's inherited his Uncle Frank's absent-mindedness. Two, he's in love."

"Frank never in his life ever kept his wallet in the oven," Marion said.

"Then Richie's in love," Howard said.

"What are we going to do?"

"Suffer, probably," Howard replied. "When I was Richie's age and I fell in love, that's what my parents did. I think we have a responsibility to carry on the tradition."

"Window shopping and looking at furniture . . . I don't like that," Marion said. "It's that Emma's fault," she said resentfully.

"Marion, I'm sure she isn't forcing Richie into window shopping. She's a nice girl. I like her."

"Yes, she *is* nice," Marion said grudgingly. "If Richie had to fall in love, why couldn't it be with some girl we didn't like? It would be so much easier. We could just tell him that—Well, we could tell him—" She sighed unhappily. "What could we tell him?"

"Nothing."

"I suppose you're right. But . . . don't you think you ought to talk to him, Howard?"

"If he *wants* to talk, yes. If he doesn't, I think I'll do what my father did when I fell in love for the first time."

"What did *he* do?"

"He told me I had my shoes on the wrong feet," Howard replied. "I've already done that for Richie."

Marion looked at him narrowly. "Who were you in love with?" she asked.

He looked off into space. "You know," he said, surprised, "I can't even remember her name."

"Oh, quit," she said. "Men always remember their first loves."

"That's in books and movies, Marion. In real life, we're all Uncle Franks—we can't even remember how we like our oatmeal, medium-rare or sunnyside up."

Stripped to the waist and awash in sweat, Richie lifted a carton of canned pumpkin from the hand truck, weaved slightly under the load, then staggered with it to the stack he was building. He dropped the carton onto the stack, then shifted it into place, making sure that it was even at all edges with the carton below it.

"There's something wrong with that," Joe Ferguson said, walking up.

"With what?" Richie asked.

"With that whole stack," Joe told him.

"What's wrong?"

"I can't put my finger on it," Joe said, "but there's something wrong."

"It's not too high for pumpkin, is it?"

Joe shook his head.

"The boxes are even, it won't fall over."

"I don't know. . . ." Joe said. He shrugged. "Oh, well. . . ." He started to walk on.

"Joe. . . ."

"Yeah?" Joe replied, halting.

"Have you got a minute?"

"Sure. Give me a box."

Richie lifted a carton from the truck and put it on the floor and Joe sat down on it.

"What's up?" Joe asked.

"I've got to have a serious talk about something," Richie said.

"Yeah, what?"

"Marriage."

"Richie," Joe said, "you came to the right guy. Because I'm going to keep you from making your first big mistake."

"Getting married? I thought you were all for it."

"No, that's not the mistake. The mistake is taking it seriously. Richie, marriage is a ball. That's where most guys goof up. The first thing they do is buy life insurance. That takes all the fun out of it. Richie—Now, listen, this is important. Life is for the living."

Richie nodded. "You told me that."

"The second thing most guys do is start a savings account," Joe said. "What for? Suppose, say, today, you go down to the bank and put ten dollars in. And tomorrow, say, you drop dead. What good is that ten dollars going to do you?"

"None, I guess."

"Right. But suppose, instead, you took that ten dollars and went out on the town? See what I mean? At least, you had a good time. They can't take that away from you, Richie."

"What I was thinking about mostly was just getting along," Richie said. "I don't make a big salary—you know that. But, I was thinking, if this girl—"

"You got a girl, Richie?"

"Sort of. If she—"

"Hot stuff, is she?" Joe asked, grinning.

Richie felt the warmth in his face. "I haven't known her a long time," he said.

"Find out, Richie," Joe advised. "That's what marriage is all about. You're not thinking straight. You've got your mind on money, Richie, when you should be asking yourself: is she hot stuff?"

"But what about renting an apartment and buying furniture and—"

"See what I mean? What do you want to do, make some landlord rich? You want to make some furniture company rich? You know what we do when the rent comes due?"

"What?"

"We go out on the town."

"You mean you don't pay the rent? What does the landlord do?"

"He calls us up. So we tell him we put the check in the mail. That keeps him off our back for a week or so. Then he calls up again. So we tell him we made an oversight, we didn't put the check in the mail, but we will now. That gets us a couple more weeks. You can keep that up. We're always two months behind. Listen, Richie, my mother didn't bring me up to make some landlord rich. See what I mean?"

"How do you buy furniture?" Richie asked.

"On time. Then you don't make the payments, then they get after you, then you make one payment—you know, just to show good faith—then you stop making payments again. By the time they come and take it away, it's used, it's no good anymore anyway. So, you go out and buy a whole new suite. On time. See how it works?"

"I don't know if I could do that," Richie said.

"Sure you could. You're no dummy. You just think you are because you don't know the ropes. All you need is to wise up."

"Thanks, anyway," Richie said.

"But, remember, find out first," Joe said.

"Find out what?"

"If she's hot stuff. You ought to meet my wife, Millie. I told her, before I ever popped the question, you got to prove it to me. You wouldn't buy a pair of shoes if you didn't try them on first, would you?"

Richie shook his head.

"Six of one, half-dozen of the other," Joe said. "Forget the money. With her working, you'll have money to burn. You know what I could do right now if I wanted to?"

"Take out a five-dollar bill and set fire to it?"

"A ten even." He got up. "It's all in the mind, Richie," he said. "You're either a high-flyer or a sitting duck. Say, here's an idea," he said. "Why don't you and me and Millie and your girl go out on a double date? What's the kid's name?"

"Emma. But I don't know—"

"I could size her up for you," Joe said. "One look, that's all I need. You ought to meet my wife, Millie, anyway. Some stuff!"

"I'll ask Emma," Richie said.

"You don't ask, you tell," Joe said. "Don't get off on the wrong foot, Richie. Let her know who wears the pants in the family. Tell her you and me and her and Millie are going out Saturday night. Millie and I know a great spot." He looked at the stack of cartons again. "Something's wrong there."

"What's the spot?" Richie asked.

"What do you care?"

"What I mean is, it isn't expensive is it?"

"You get paid, don't you?"

"I'm saving up, though—for college."

"Richie, make up your mind," Joe said. "What do you want to do, go to college or have a ball? You can't go to college and get married. You can't buy anything on time if you're a college kid. You got to have a job. Listen, how's this? Saturday night is on me."

"No, I wouldn't want you to do that."

"If I can set fire to it, I can spend it on my best buddy, can't I?"

Richie looked at him in surprise; he hadn't realized that he and Joe Ferguson were that close.

"Well, I guess I could dip into my savings this once," Richie said.

"No. It's on me." He pointed to the stack. "That's what's wrong with it," he said. "That's pumpkins."

"Yeah. . . ."

"You're in canned corn," Joe told him. "Pumpkins are over in the next aisle."

Richie drooped.

"See you Saturday," Joe said, going on.

Drearily, Richie set to work to dismantle the stack.

Trudging through the park on his way home that evening, Richie came upon a group of his friends playing a pick-up game of baseball. One was pitching, one was batting, one was playing the infield and the other three were in the outfield. Worn out after the long walk from the warehouse, Richie sat down on the grass and watched. After a few minutes, his friend Potsie came in from the outfield and sat down beside him.

"Want to hit some?" Potsie asked.

"I couldn't lift the bat."

"That must be a tough job."

"I'm getting kind of used to that," Richie told him. "But I just walked all the way in. It must be a thousand miles."

"What happened to the bus?"

"No money," Richie told him. "I guess I lost my wallet. I know I had it with me when I left the house this morning. The last thing I did was get it out of my mother's kitchen drawer. But when I got off work I couldn't find it."

"It'll turn up," Potsie said optimistically. "Did you have much in it?"

Richie shook his head. "Just a couple bucks. Did you go on that camp-out with the girls?" he asked.

"That didn't work out," Potsie replied.

"How're the things out at the beach?"

"Confused," Potsie told him.

"What do you mean?"

"You know Jack and Sally, how they were going together?"

"I didn't know that."

Potsie nodded. "They started just before school let out," he said. "But now already, Jack is going with Marlene. I was going to start going with Sally, but before I could even get revved up, she was going with Tom. I didn't even know they liked each other. Tom always used to say her teeth stuck out."

"I guess he changed his mind. But what's confusing?"

"Betty isn't going with Mitch anymore, either. Mitch is going with Alice now—since Tom switched over to Sally."

"When was Tom going with Alice?"

"Before Sally."

"I can figure that out—but when was he going with Alice? I didn't know about it. I thought he was going with What's-her-name . . . you know, the one with all the hair."

"Susie," Potsy said. "He only went with her a couple days, though, then he started going with Alice."

"What's Betty doing now?" Richie asked.

"Gerald."

"Louise?"

"Bill. But I think they're breaking up. He's been

hanging around Mary Lou. He ducked her in the surf twice yesterday. So Louise went home with Carl Nesbit."

"That gets confusing," Richie said.

"The whole world all of a sudden," Potsie said, "is turned upside down. I used to know who everybody was going with. Now, the only thing I know is: I'm not going with anybody. You're lucky you've got that job, you're out of it."

"Yeah, and I've got Em—" Richie fell suddenly silent.

"Got what?"

"Nothing."

"You said 'em' something."

"I forgot what I was going to say."

They watched the ball playing for a while in silence.

Then Potsie said, "Girls are all alike. If I ever find one to go with, I'm going to keep her on a short leash. You can't trust them."

"Some you can," Richie said.

"Name one."

"It works both ways, though," Richie said. "You can't be playing the field yourself and expect them not to. You have to have an understanding . . . sort of an agreement . . . or married or something."

"Yeah, but who wants to get married?"

"Some guys do."

"Older guys, yeah. But I'm talking about us."

"Some guys mature faster than others," Richie said.

"Nobody I know," Potsie said, getting up. "My turn at bat," he said, leaving.

Richie watched for another few minutes, then rose and trudged on. He began to realize how fortunate he was, having Emma. It was nice not to have to worry about losing her. She didn't know anybody else but him. That wouldn't last forever, though. When school started in the fall, she'd get to know everybody. And, boy, being the new girl in town, every guy in the school would make a bee line for her. Jack. Tom. Mitch. Gerald. Bill. Carl Nesbit. Potsie, too, the traitor.

That night at the Watt house, helping Emma roll up the living room rug so that her mother could see how the room would look without it, Richie asked her if she would like to double date.

"Sure," she replied enthusiastically. "I was beginning to wonder if I was ever going to meet *any*body."

"This is a guy at work," Richie said.

"What's he like?"

"Older," Richie said.

She seemed disappointed. "Ancient?" she asked.

"No, about twenty or something."

"Oh, that's all right. That boy I told you about who wanted me to go to his homecoming was nineteen. Does *your* friend go to college?"

"He works."

"What does he look like?"

"Tall guy, kind of skinny."

"Like James Stewart?"

Richie shook his head. "More like Bugs Bunny," he said. "But normal ears."

"He sounds cute," Emma said excitedly.

"He's married," Richie told her.

"Oh." She turned and called toward the back of the house. "Mother! It's rolled up! Come look!"

"His wife's name is Millie," Richie said.

"That's nice," Emma said indifferently. She called out again. "Mothhhhhher!"

"She works, too," Richie said. "They make out real great that way, both of them having jobs. According to what Joe says, it's a real ball."

Emma's interest suddenly revived. "Does he talk about being married?" she asked.

"He almost doesn't talk about anything else." He lowered his eyes. "They've got an apartment," he said. "They live there together. Just them."

"Remember that living room set we saw last night," Emma said. "Wouldn't that go nice in an apartment? It's just the right size."

"The one where the couch folds out?"

She nodded. "And makes a bed."

"It'd be the right size, all right," Richie agreed.

"We could have— I mean, if somebody had it in an apartment, they could have six little pictures right behind it on the wall. With red frames. I saw that in *Better Homes & Gardens.*"

"I wonder where your mother is?" Richie said, looking toward the hall.

"And that coffee table that looks like a cobbler's bench," Emma said. "It could be right in front of the couch."

"You'd have to move it when you pulled the . . . the, you know, the bed out."

"Oh, sure."

Mrs. Watt arrived. Looking at the bare floor, she made a face of extreme anguish.

"You don't like it." Emma guessed.

"There's so *much* floor," Mrs. Watt said.

"It was under the rug," Richie told her.

"Much too much," Mrs. Watt said. "Put the rug back, dears," she said, sweeping from the room.

"You know what I'd like to see in an apartment?" Richie said to Emma. "An all linoleum floor."

FOUR

"That's the city line we just crossed," Joe Ferguson announced to Richie and Emma, in the back seat of his car.

"Across that line, it's a different world, if you know what I mean," Millie, Joe's wife, said. Millie was a tall, slender girl, with henna-tinted hair and enormous eyes that never seemed to blink.

"What *do* you mean?" Emma asked, somewhat nervously.

"The sky's the limit," Joe answered.

"When you cross that line, you leave your P's and Q's behind, if you know what I mean," Millie said.

Emma whispered to Richie. "What do they mean?"

He shrugged. "I don't know—if you know what I mean."

A short while later, Joe turned the car from the highway and into a parking area that surrounded a king-size quonset hut, a building with a rounded roof. The parking area was crowded, and couples, having left their cars, were making their way toward the building. The muted sound of a band could be heard.

"Ooooooo!" Millie said excitedly. "Can't you just feel it!"

"What?" Richie asked.

"It's just cray-zeee!" she told him.

Joe parked the car and they got out and joined the other couples who were converging on the quonset hut. Richie and Emma hung back a few steps.

"It's a roadhouse, I think," Emma said. "Richie, are you sure they'll let us in? I don't think we're old enough."

"On this side of the city line, I guess we are," Richie told her.

They reached the entrance. A heavy-set man, with a flat, mashed face, wearing a tuxedo, was standing just inside. He looked at Richie and Emma as if he intended to speak to them.

"It's okay, Bruno, they're with me," Joe told the man.

Bruno nodded and the foursome proceeded.

The interior was dimly-lighted, smoky and jammed. In the center there was a small dance floor. Bunched in around it on three sides were tables. At the far end there was a long, crowded bar. The band, on a small stand not far from the entrance, was playing a jump tune, and the dance floor was alive with jumpers.

"Ooooooo!" Millie said again, throbbing with anticipation. "Isn't it cool!"

Richie fanned cigarette smoke from in front of his eyes.

Joe led the way to a table. When they were seated, he caught a passing waitress by an apron string, and, when she was thus forced to stop, ordered four beers. The waitress looked questioningly at Richie and Emma.

"I fixed it with Bruno," Joe told her.

That appeared to satisfy her; she moved on.

"I'll show you the little girls' room," Millie said to Emma.

They left the table and disappeared into the haze of smoke.

"Is this class or is this class?" Joe said to Richie, grinning.

"Boy!"

"Remember—it's on me," Joe told him.

"No, I brought money."

"How much?"

"I didn't know how much it would be, so I brought it all," Richard told him.

"Sharp," Joe said. "But, forget it, Richie—it's on me." He leaned forward. "I like that Emma," he said. "You're in like Flynn, buddy-boy. I can tell." He winked. "In the words of the song, she's only got eyes for you. Get what I mean?"

"Millie's nice too," Richie said.

"Hot stuff, isn't she? Fast on the uptake, too. It runs in the family. She's not Charles M. Coogan's niece for nothing."

"I've never seen him," Richie said.

"I'll take you into his office and introduce you someday," Joe told him. He entwined two fingers. "Charles M. Coogan and me are just like that."

Emma and Millie returned.

"Let's trip the light fantastic, hot stuff," Joe said to Millie, rising.

With Millie giggling, they headed toward the dance floor.

"Is this class or is this class?" Richie said to Emma, when Joe and his wife had gone.

"My eyes burn," she said.

"Mine, too."

The waitress delivered the four beers, then hustled away.

Richie peered at the beer for a second, then looked at Emma. Emma was looking at him.

She leaned toward him and whispered, "I've only had beer once before."

"It's nothing," he told her. "Go ahead."

"You go."

Richie picked up his stein and sipped. "Nothing," he repeated.

Emma sipped. She made a face. "I think it's sour," she said.

"No, that's the way it tastes. You've got a mustache," he told her.

Emma wiped the foam from her upper lip.

"Want to dance?" Richie asked.

"Not yet."

They looked toward the dance floor. Joe and Millie were bouncing about in wild abandon.

"They're a lot of fun, aren't they?" Emma said.

"Uh-huh. But why not? They've got everything anybody could want—that car, and all the money they can use, and they've got a whole apartment all by themselves." He sipped his beer again. "That's really living."

"Wouldn't it be wonderful!"

Joe and Millie returned.

"Bottoms up!" Joe said, raising his stein.

"Down the hatch!" Millie said.

Richie and Emma watched in fascination as the beer drained from the mugs.

Joe banged the empty stein on the stable. "Set 'em

up in the other aisle, toots!" he shouted out to the passing waitress. He saw that Richie's and Emma's mugs were still nearly full. "What's the matter, gang?" he said. "On the wagon?"

"We're just warming up," Richie told him.

"Don't miss the boat, if you know what I mean," Millie said. She broke into another spasm of giggles.

"I told you, didn't I?" Joe said to Richie. "Is she fast on the uptake?"

"Boy, yeah," Richie said.

Joe looped an arm around Millie's shoulders and whispered into her ear. Millie exploded in hysterics.

"I'd tell you what I told her," Joe said to Richie and Emma, "but it's a little risque." He winked at Emma. "Know what I mean?"

Emma blushed and looked down at her stein of beer..

"There's a slow number," Joe said, getting up. "Come on, hot stuff, let's wrestle," he said to Millie.

She bounced up and they departed toward the dance floor.

"Want to yet?" Richie asked Emma.

She nodded and they rose and followed Joe and Millie.

As Richie and Emma danced—a bit stiffly—Richie kept his eyes on Joe and Millie. They were pressed so tightly together that they seemed to be a part of each other. They kissed almost continuously. Watching, Richie kept clearing his throat, feeling embarrassed—but also envious.

When the slow tune ended and the band broke into another jump number, Richie and Emma returned to the table. The waitress had delivered four more beers.

"I was just getting started with the first one," Emma said.

"Me, too. Well . . ."

They sat watching Joe and Millie on the dance floor.

"This is fun," Emma said. But she was not convincing.

"I'm having a great time," Richie said.

"But I can't stay out too late."

"Okay."

Soon, Joe and Millie returned.

"Emma can't stay out too late," Richie told them.

Joe nudged Millie. "Did you hear that, toots? Emma can't stay out too late!"

"Oh, Joe!" Millie said, breaking into whoops of laughter.

"Bottoms up!" Joe said, raising his stein.

The rest of the evening was a repeat. Joe and Millie distributed their time about evenly between the dance floor and the table. Richie and Emma danced the slow numbers and sat out the fast ones. When they were all at the table, Millie was in a constant state of unrestrained glee. Joe was putting away his own and Richie's and Emma's beers.

At eleven, Emma told Richie that she thought they ought to start home.

When informed, Joe was disappointed. "In the words of the song, the night is young," he said.

Millie was provoked once more to giggling laughter.

"Yeah, but we have to go," Richie said.

Joe stopped the waitress and asked for the check. She ripped it from the pad she carried and handed it to him. Joe reached toward his hip pocket. He frowned. He began patting his other pockets.

"Son of a gun," Joe said. "You know what I did?"

"Left your money in your other pants," the waitress said dryly.

"Is that dumb or is that dumb?" Joe said.

"Joe, you never did that before," Millie said, seeming to come in on cue.

"There's a first time for everything."

"Oh, Joe!" Whooping laughter.

"Get this, will you, Richie," Joe said, passing the check to him. "You'll get it back tomorrow, first thing."

Richie took the check and looked at it. His eyes widened. "Wow!"

"You want me to get Bruno?" the waitress said to Joe.

"No, the kid can handle it."

Richie got his money from his pocket and put two ten-dollar bills on the table.

The waitress waited.

"I'm a big tipper, Richie," Joe said. "Slip her a fiver."

Painfully, Richie obeyed, then they left.

"Don't forget what I owe you," Joe said to Richie, as they walked toward the car. "You know how I am about money—in one pocket and out the other. Funny, how I forgot my billfold."

"I do that, too," Richie told him.

On the way back to town, in the rear seat, Richie put an arm around Emma and she snuggled close to him and they talked quietly.

"They're lucky," Emma said. "When they get home they'll still be together."

"And that's not all," Richie said.

"What else?"

Richie was thinking about Joe's comment that he

and Millie risqued all over the apartment. But he could not quite bring himself to use the word with Emma.

"I mean they're married," he said.

"Oh." Evidently she understood.

"Listen, I was thinking," Richie said. "We don't go out with anybody else anyway. How would you like to go steady?"

"I guess we could do that," she replied. She turned her head slightly and kissed his cheek. "I'd like that."

Richie turned toward her.

But Joe intervened. "Are you sure you two want to duck out?" he called back to them. "Millie and me know a lot more great spots."

"No, I think we better," Richie replied.

They reached the Watt house a short while later. Goodnights were said, then Joe and Millie drove on and Richie and Emma walked toward the porch.

"It really was a lot of fun," Emma said.

"Yeah, it was a ball."

They reached the door and Emma opened it, then paused.

"It's kind of late," she said.

Richie nodded.

"We're going steady now, though," Emma said. "So if you want to come in for a minute, I guess it would be all right."

"Well, okay."

They stepped into the entryway. The rest of the house appeared to be dark.

From upstairs, a voice called down. Mrs. Watt. "Emma? Is that you?"

"Yes, Mother."

"Aren't you a little late?"

"Sorry."

"All right."

Emma whispered to Richie. "She doesn't know we're going steady yet."

"Yeah, she couldn't know."

"Shhhh!"

"Okay," Richie whispered.

"I wonder if Joe and Millie went to some other spot," Emma said.

"I don't know. Probably. But maybe they didn't."

Again, from upstairs, the voice. "Emma—is someone with you?"

"Richie, Mother. We're talking."

"Don't talk too long."

"We won't."

"Goodnight, Richie," Mrs. Watt called down.

"Goodnight."

Emma whispered again. "At least, Joe and Millie don't have someone telling them how long they can talk," she said.

"Boy, no."

"They're *really* lucky."

Richie nodded.

"I've never gone steady before," Emma said.

"Me, neither. Well . . . not steady steady. I did once for about two days, but I was just a kid then."

"Oh, well, I did, too, once, like that," Emma said. "But I mean I haven't ever when it counted—like this." She smiled softly. "It's nice."

"The guys won't believe it," Richie said.

"I guess you'll have to introduce me," Emma said.

Richie thought about Jack and Sally and Tom and Alice and—or was it Mitch and Alice?—and Gerald and Louise—no, it was Gerald and Betty, wasn't it? —and—

"There's plenty of time for that," he said.

"But if you tell them about me and they don't know me, won't they wonder?"

"Wonder what?"

"I don't know, just wonder."

"Have you got a picture?" Richie asked.

From upstairs once more, the voice. "Emma, I don't hear anything."

"Mother, I told you, we're just talking."

"Why don't I hear you talking?"

"We're talking low, we don't want to keep you awake."

"Don't be too long."

"Yes, Mother."

"I guess I better go," Richie said to Emma.

"I guess," she agreed.

Richie reached out hesitantly. Then they were in each other's arms, with their mouths mashed together, the same as the first time. The kiss continued for a long minute. They came up for a breath, then pressed together again. This time, the kiss was less frantic.

From upstairs: "Emma—I can't hear you again."

The embrace continued.

"Emma? Is Richie still there?"

Emma pried Richie loose. "Goodnight," she said breathlessly.

Then she ran up the stairs.

Richie remained standing in the entryway, looking up the stairway, for a few moments after she had gone. He felt grossly unsatisfied. As before, the kiss had promised so much, and he was left, literally, empty-handed. Then, still feeling somehow cheated, he left the house.

Walking up the block, he thought about Joe and Millie again. They had probably gone on to the apartment instead of to another nightspot. That was what he and Emma would do, he was sure, if they were Joe and Millie. That would really be swell, having a place where they could be alone—with nobody calling down the stairs to them. It would be everything. Who could want anything more?

Richie saw that the light was on in the kitchen when he got home. He walked quietly toward the back of the house, and as he neared the kitchen he heard his parents' voices. They were talking in low tones. Perhaps it was something private. Approaching the doorway, he halted.

"That's what we owe the dentist," Howard Cunningham said.

"Couldn't he wait?" Marion suggested.

"He probably could," Howard replied. "But when I called him up with that tooth, he didn't ask *me* to wait."

"I suppose you're right. Well, look, we could put off the new washing machine. It isn't that desperate."

"Marion, the only thing holding that old washer together is fatigue. It's too tired to fall apart."

"I can manage."

"How? By taking our clothes down to the river and beating them against a rock?"

Richie coughed—deliberately.

"Richie?" his father called.

He went into the kitchen. "Hi," he said cheerily. "Burning the midnight oil?"

"No, we're sitting here under the electric light," Howard Cunningham replied.

"I sort of heard you talking a little bit," Richie said, sobering. "If you need some money, I've got some, you know. Not as much as I had—but some."

"Richie, did you lose your wallet again?" his mother asked.

"No. Emma and I double dated with this guy at work and his wife tonight," he explained, "and I had to pay. He was supposed to, but, by accident, he forgot his billfold."

"Left it in his other trousers?" Howard said.

"How did you know that?"

"A lucky guess."

"He's going to pay me back—if you need the money," Richie said.

"Dear, that's sweet," his mother said. "But it isn't necessary. Your father and I were just trying to figure out if we can all go on a vaction trip this year without taking any money out of savings."

"Savings?"

"You know," his father said, "the way ants store up nuts."

"That squirrels, Dad." He sat down at the table. "What are you worried about savings for?" he said. "You ought to be enjoying life while you can. If you want to take a trip, take a trip. What good will savings do you when you're six feet under?"

Marion Cunningham turned quickly to her husband. "Howard, are you ill? Why didn't you tell me!"

"I'm not ill," he replied. "Or, if I am, it's news to me."

"Why did you say your father was ill?" Marion asked

her son. "Richie, don't ever do that again. You gave me such a start."

"Mom, I didn't mean dad. I'm talking about everybody."

"We're all sick?" Howard asked. "Is this a family epidemic or is the whole world in on it?"

"I'm talking about staying home if you want to take a trip," Richie said. "What good is the money going to do you after you're dead? I don't mean just you. I mean everybody. Life is for the living."

His parents looked at each other.

Howard Cunningham faced Richie again. "Life is for the living?" he said. "Is that something new? What was life for before? The dead?"

"You're not living, you and Mom," Richie told him. "Do you know what you're doing? You're making the dentist rich."

"I don't think I could come up with enough cavities for that, Richie. Well-to-do, maybe. But not rich."

"You don't understand what I'm saying. What I mean is, money isn't important, only love is."

Howard Cunningham brightened. "Ahhh . . . love. . . . Now, I understand."

Marion smiled. "Yes, why didn't you say that in the beginning, dear?"

Richie beamed. "I didn't think it would be that easy," he said. "But, now that you see, where are you going on the trip?"

"We're not sure we're going, dear," his mother replied. "It depends on whether we can do it without taking money out of savings. I explained that."

Richie sagged. "You didn't really understand," he

said. "Don't you see, as long as you have love, as long as you have each other, saving isn't important."

"As long as we have each other?" his father said.

"Sure."

"Richie, suppose a big, unexpected expense comes up and I don't have any money in savings? What do I do, send them your mother?"

Richie peered at him.

"If I did that, I wouldn't have her any longer," Howard Cunningham said. "And if I didn't have her, we wouldn't have each other any more." He shook his head. "It think I'll stick to savings, Richie, if you don't mind."

"I was just trying to help," Richie said.

"Thanks, anyway."

"Shouldn't you be in bed, dear?" his mother said.

"Mom, I'm not a baby."

"All right."

"I'm a little tired, though," he said. "I guess I will go up." He rose. "Oh . . . I'm going steady," he said.

His mother flinched.

"Emma?" Howard Cunningham asked.

Richie nodded.

"She seems like a very nice girl," Howard said.

Richie nodded again. "Goodnight." Then he left.

"It's getting serious, Howard," Marion said, when Richie had gone.

"We'll see."

"No, I'm worried. You heard how he was talking."

"Marion, I talked that way, too, when I was his age. I was just as positive then as he is now that love was the solution to everything. In fact, I'm still convinced that it is. It's the dentist who's a non-believer."

"What will we do if it gets *more* serious?"

"Trade him in on a new washing machine," Howard replied. "Then it'll be the appliance store's problem."

"You can joke, but I really am worried."

"I know you are, Marion. That's your nature. But, think back—in all the years, has worrying ever helped?"

"No. . . ." she admitted. "But I don't feel as guilty if I worry."

"You have no reason to feel guilty. If it turns into a problem, it won't be your fault."

"Maybe we could send him away for the rest of the summer."

"I suspect that no matter where we send him, he would find an Emma," Howard said. "He's reached that age." He suddenly frowned and looked off into space.

"Did you think of something?" Marion asked hopefully.

"Yes. For one thing, I think we could put off painting the porches for another year. That would save us enough for a short trip—say to the edge of town."

FIVE

The hand truck was piled high. But Richie was having no trouble moving it. He and the hand truck were sailing along the main aisle, headed for the rear of the warehouse. The ease with which they were traveling was due to the fact that the truck was loaded with cartons of cornflakes.

Ahead, Mr. Starch, the supervisor, appeared from an aisle and stopped and looked in one direction and then the other, and then focused on Richie and the truck. He raised a hand, indicating to Richie that he wanted him to halt. Richie dug in, dragging the truck to a slow stop.

"Where's Joe Ferguson?" Mr. Starch asked.

"I haven't seen him in a couple days," Richie replied. "He's here, though, I know. Every day I ask for him. And somebody's always seen him. But I can never find him."

"Aren't you supposed to be getting orders from him?" the supervisor asked.

"Yes, sir."

"Who's been giving you orders?"

"Nobody," Richie replied. "I figure out what to do myself."

Starch raised his eyebrows. "You mean you just go ahead and do your work without being told?"

Richie nodded. "It doesn't take much brains," he said. "The trucks unload and the stuff has to be put away. When that's all there is to do, who needs to be told?"

"You'd be surprised how many people have to be told," Starch said. He motioned, indicating that Richie could proceed, then, when Richie and the truck moved on, he walked beside them. "I like your attitude, Cunningham," he said. "What do you want to do in life?"

"Do?"

"Work."

"I haven't decided, sir. First, I have to finish high school. Then, I've been thinking about going on to college."

"Any chance you might change your mind?"

"About college? I don't know."

"Do you know what business we're in here, Cunningham?" Starch said.

"Yes, sir. Grocery supply."

"That's what it looks like, yes," the supervisor said. "But, the fact is, Cunningham, we're in the happiness business. Take these cornflakes. What if we weren't here to get these cornflakes from the manufacturer and then move them on to the stores? Thousands of people would wake up in the morning and go down to breakfast and find themselves without their cornflakes. They'd be pretty damn unhappy about that, don't you think?"

"Yes, sir," Richie replied, turning the truck into an aisle.

"Happiness makes the world go round, Cunningham. If a man isn't happy, pretty soon he stops going to work. Maybe he even takes up with drink. If the men don't go to work, the factories stop. The whole *system* stops, Cunningham."

"Yes, sir," Richie said again.

"I like to think that we're helping to keep the system going," the supervisor said. "We're putting the cornflakes on the breakfast table that keeps the man happy and keeps him on his job and keeps the wheels turning."

Richie stopped the truck at the cereal section.

"Think about it," Starch said. "We could use a boy like you here at Mid-State. You've got get-up-and-go. Not like that Ferguson." He looked around. "When I find that— I'm not going to put up with his lazy ways forever. I don't care if he is related to the Big Boss. It's only by marriage—he better remember that."

"Joe's probably working," Richie said. "He's just not right around here, that's all."

"He hasn't worked since the day he set foot in this place."

Richie began building a stack of cornflakes cartons.

"What I need in his job is somebody like you, somebody with your attitude," Starch said. "Think about what I told you. You might decide to stay on when summer ends. School's all right. But, you know, I didn't finish high school and look at me. I've got fourteen men under me. If you've got the right attitude, you can go right to the top in this business, Cunningham."

Richie paused, holding a carton of cornflakes. "Do you really think so?"

"Look at me," Starch said. "Where's there a better example?"

Richie placed the carton on the stack.

"If you see that Joe Ferguson, tell him I want him

in my office," the supervisor said. Then he departed, walking back along the aisle, looking to the right and to the left, his head cocked, as if trying to pick up Joe Ferguson's scent.

Richie continued stacking cartons. But a short while after the supervisor had gone, his attention was caught by a scraping sound. He looked around and saw nothing out of the ordinary. As he resumed work, however, he heard the sound again. This time, out of a corner of an eye, he also saw movement. A tall carton at the end of the aisle had shifted.

Richie peered at the carton, waiting for it to move again. That expectation was soon satisfied. The box rocked and nearly fell over on its side. It became still again. Then the shaking resumed. After a minute, Joe Ferguson began emerging from the carton—the top of his head, then his eyes, bleary, looking over the rim. At last, his whole head and shoulders appeared.

"Is the coast clear?" Joe asked, his voice unusually husky.

"There's nobody here but me," Richie replied.

Joe began rocking the carton back and forth. Finally, it fell forward and landed with a loud whap. Joe crawled out.

"What a night!" he moaned, rising. He blinked his eyes painfully. "Ever drink boilermakers?" he asked Richie.

"I don't think so."

"If you ever get the chance, don't do it," Joe advised. "Wow! My head feels like it's on inside out."

"Mr. Starch is looking for you," Richie told him.

Joe shrugged. "Let him look," he said.

"He's kind of mad."

"What do I care?" He entwined two fingers. "Me and Charles W. Coogan," he said.

"Joe. . . ." Richie said. "Remember that Saturday night when you and me and Millie and Emma went out? You left your money in your other pants, remember?"

Ferguson looked at him foggily. "I remember going out," he said.

"Yeah. And I had to pay the bill. You said it was on you, but— Well. . . . I don't expect you to pay the whole thing, but could I have your half?"

"What do you mean, I didn't pay you? That's not like me, Richie."

"You didn't, though."

"All right, if you say so. It's your word against mine, but I'm not the kind of guy that makes a mountain out of molehill." He reached for his back pocket. "We'll settle up right now. What do I owe you?"

"Ten'll be fair," Richie said.

Joe looked suddenly surprised. "You know what I did? I think I did it again," he said. "I went off without my billfold. Is that dumb, or is that dumb?"

Richie didn't answer.

"Tell you what I'll do, I'll put a check in the mail to you the minute I get home tonight," Joe said.

"You don't have to do that. Just bring the ten in tomorrow."

"Or, I could do it that way," Joe replied agreeably. "You look me up tomorrow," he said, heading off down the aisle.

"You going in to see Mr. Starch?" Richie asked.

"I'm going to find a better box," Joe replied. "That

one didn't have any packing in it. It was like sleeping on cement."

As Richie arrived at the Watt house that evening, Emma's parents were leaving, going to a movie.

"Why don't you and Emma come with us?" Mrs. Watt suggested.

"I like to rest my eyes at night," Richie said.

"What, dear?"

"The light isn't too good at the warehouse and I do a lot of squinting during the day," Richie explained.

Mrs. Watt looked perplexed, but she didn't pursue the subject. She and Mr. Watt left the house and got into the family car and drove away. When they had gone, Richie walked toward the kitchen, looking for Emma. He found her there, washing the dinner dishes. He got a towel from the rack and began drying.

"You didn't want to go to a movie, did you?" Richie said. "Your mom and dad offered."

"I'd rather stay at home."

"That's what I thought. Where's Bobs?" he asked.

"Around. Upstairs, I think. Or down the basement."

When they finished the dishes, they went into the living room.

"The reason I didn't want to go to the movie was, I wanted to rest my eyes," Richie said.

Emma did not question him. "If it's too bright in here, I could turn off some of the lights," she said.

"That might be a good idea," Richie said, settling on the sofa.

Emma went from lamp to lamp, switching them off. When the room was dark except for the spillover from the light in the entryway, she joined Richie on the sofa.

They were in each other's arms almost before she could get seated. A bruising kiss began—but was immediately interrupted.

Emma's brother, Bobs, came into the room. "What're all the lights off for?" he asked. "Emma, is that you?"

Richie and Emma quickly separated.

"Richie's resting his eyes," Emma told her brother. "What do you want?"

Bobbs turned on a lamp. He was carrying what Richie recognized as an automobile fuel pump.

"Want to buy this?" Bobs asked Richie.

"What would I do with it?"

"It's good junk," Bobs said. "See how I cleaned it up?"

"Good job," Richie said.

"I'll sell it to you for fifty cents."

"It looks like it's shot," Richie said.

"It is. I got it at the filling station. They threw it away."

"What would I want with it?" Richie asked.

"Don't you like junk?" Bobs replied. "I could get a dollar for this, I bet. But you can have it for fifty cents."

"Bobs, Richie doesn't want that thing," Emma said crossly. "Haven't you got something to do?"

"I'm doing it—selling junk," he replied. He faced Richie again. "You can have it for thirty-five cents," he said.

"Can you really sell that stuff?" Richie asked.

"Sure. It's good junk."

"But it's junk."

"Not after I clean it up," Bobs said. He held up the fuel pump. "Look at the way that shines. Can you see it? The light's not good enough," he said. He began going from lamp to lamp, turning them all on. "Wait'll you can really see this," he said. "It'll knock your eyes out."

"Want to go for a walk?" Richie said to Emma. "We could go over to the park."

She nodded. "Let's go for a walk."

"Don't you want to see this?" Bobs called after them as they departed. "Want me to come with you?"

Emma halted. "If you do, I'll kill you," she told her brother.

Bobs gestured indifferently. "All right . . . if you don't like junk," he said.

Richie and Emma left the house and, hand in hand, walked the several blocks to the park, then sat down on a bench near the statue of the Civil War general.

"It's nice here," Emma said.

"I like the way that tree hides the moon," Richie said. "I hope Bobs doesn't come along and chop it down."

Emma laughed, then rested against him. Richie slipped an arm around her and drew her close.

They heard a throat being cleared. Looking up, they saw a policeman standing a few steps away.

"Beautiful evening," the policeman said.

Richie removed his arm from around Emma. "We were just talking about that," he said.

"Good for walking," the policeman said.

"That's how we got here—walked," Emma told him.

"Can't ever get enough walking," the policeman said. "It's good for the blood."

Richie and Emma got up and walked on, with the policeman trailing leisurely after them.

"Maybe a movie's not such a bad idea, after all," Richie said. "Want to?"

"What's on?"

"Who cares?"

Emma laughed again. "All right, let's."

They walked into town and stopped at the first movie they came to, a Betty Hutton film. The back row of seats in the theater, unfortunately, was filled, but they were able to find two side-by-side places in the next-to-the-back row. On the screen, Betty Hutton was belting out a song. Again, Richie put an arm around Emma. She snuggled close.

"Indecent!" a voice behind them hissed.

Richic and Emma separated and looked back. A middle-aged woman was leaning forward, glaring at them.

"Any more of that and I'll call the manager!" the woman told them.

"What'd we do?" Richie asked puzzledly.

"Shhhh!" the man next to him said.

"I know necking when I see it," the woman told Richie.

"Shhhh!" the man said to her.

"We just sat down," Richie said.

"Shhhh!" the man said to him.

"Nobody's going to neck in any movie I'm in," the woman told Richie. "You try that again and I'll call the manager, I swear."

"Shhhh!"

"Let's go," Richie said to Emma.

They left the theater and, glum, walked back toward the Watt house.

"Why can't people leave people alone?" Emma said resentfully.

Richie shrugged.

"We weren't doing anything."

He nodded.

"Joe and Millie don't have to put up with anything like that, that's one thing," Emma said. "If they want to be alone, nobody goes around saying they're indecent."

"They're married, though," Richie pointed out.

"That's not *everything.*"

"I know. It doesn't make that much difference to me, either," Richie said. "But to a lot of people it does. I don't think you could get an apartment if you weren't married, could you?"

"I suppose not. They probably make you show them the license."

"There are a *lot* of things you can do when you're married," Richie said.

She looked at him sideways. "What?"

Richie thought. "Well. . . . Anything."

"Oh."

They were silent, thinking their own private thoughts, most of the way to the Watt house.

Emma's parents were at home when Richie and Emma got there. They were in the kitchen, having hot cocoa.

"You should have gone with us," Mrs. Watt said to Richie and Emma. "Elizabeth Taylor was lovely. She was so beautiful, I cried."

"Last week, you cried at the bombing of Berlin," Mr. Watt said.

"Not in the same way."

"Daddy, how can you drink hot cocoa in this weather?" Emma asked.

"I always have hot cocoa before I go to bed."

"But it must be eighty degrees out."

"I still have to sleep, don't I? I can't sleep if I don't have my hot cocoa."

"The wedding was lovely, too," Mrs. Watt said.

"Who got married?" Richie asked.

"Elizabeth Taylor. Poor Spencer Tracy."

"Isn't he a little old for her?" Richie asked.

"He was her father, dear. She married— I don't remember who she married. But he looked like a very nice young man." She beamed. "I love weddings."

"I liked the bombing of Berlin," Mr. Watt said.

Richie and Emma left them and went into the living room and sat down on the sofa.

"They'll be going to bed soon," Emma said.

"I had a serious talk with Mr. Starch, the supervisor at work, today," Richie told her. "He says I could really go a long way there."

"How far?" Emma asked, interested.

"I don't think I'm going to be running the place real soon. But I think he's going to try to fire Joe, and—"

"Oh, Richie, that's terrible."

"I know. But Joe goofs off a lot. Millie's the Big Boss's niece, though, so I don't know what'll happen. I might even be put *over* Joe."

"Gee!"

"If I stayed there," Richie said. "But I guess I'll be going back to school in fall. Unless I didn't want to."

"How could you go to college if you didn't go back to high school?"

"There are other things in life than college. Look at

Mr. Starch, he didn't even finish high school and he supervises the whole works. But, even if I got Joe's job, I don't know how much money it would be. Millie works, too, you know. That's how Joe can just take out a ten-dollar bill if he wants to and burn it."

"I don't know *why* I'm going back to school," Emma said. "I ought to get a job like Millie."

Emma's parents appeared in the entryway. Mr. Watt went on up the stairs, but Mrs. Watt lingered.

"Don't be too long, Emma," she said.

"We're just talking," Emma said.

Mrs. Watt entered the room and turned on the one lamp that was not burning. "I don't know how you children can see in the dark," she said. "You'll ruin your eyes."

"Mother, we're not reading, we're talking."

"Well, Richie has bad eyes, anyway."

"No, I don't."

"You told me tonight you couldn't go to the movie because you had to rest them."

"They're not bad, though. They just get tired. Anyway, they're rested now."

"Then they'll like the light," Mrs. Watt said, going toward the entryway. "Eyes *like* light, Richie. They feed on it. You wouldn't plant new grass seed and not give it all the fertilizer it needs, would you?" She paused. "Remember, now, Emma—not too late."

"All right, mother."

Mrs. Watt went up the stairs.

"What have my eyes got to do with grass seed?" Richie asked.

"She thinks those things up," Emma told him. She rose and turned off two of the lamps, leaving one on, then returned to the sofa. "I don't know what she thinks we're going to do, anyway," she said testily. "You'd think we were children."

"What would you do if you got a job?" Richie asked.

"I don't know. I've never thought about it."

"Millie works at the telephone company."

"I could do that," Emma said enthusiastically. "When you think about it, why should I finish school? Someday . . . I don't know when, but someday, I'll be getting married. And who cares what the date of the Mexican-American War was then?"

"I thought you wanted to go to college."

"I thought you did, too."

"That was before," Richie said. "I've learned a lot this summer. Maybe I matured too fast and matured right on past college. I've got a lot of experience at Mid-State, too, don't forget. Why give it all up?"

There were footfalls on the stairs.

Emma leaped up and switched on the two lights that she had turned off.

Mr. Watt appeared and stopped at the entrance to the living room. "Your mother thinks she left the gas on in the kitchen," he said. "Just checking." He moved on.

"I'll bet!" Emma said.

"I wonder what an apartment costs," Richie said.

"I wouldn't have any idea."

"It wouldn't be too much—for two people with jobs," Richie said. "Because look at Joe and Millie. They don't always pay their rent on time, but that's because they go out on the town a lot, I think. We—I mean, two people wouldn't *have* to go out all the time.

And they wouldn't *have* to have a car right away, like Joe and Millie."

"There's furniture," Emma said.

"You can get that on time."

Mr. Watt returned. "It's okay, it was turned off," he reported.

"Daddie, tell mother all we're doing is talking," Emma said.

He looked at her blankly. "What?"

"Oh, never mind."

"You kids. . . ." Mr. Watt said, heading for the stairs.

When he had gone, Emma got up and turned off the lights again.

"I was thinking . . . ," Richie said, when Emma was settled on the sofa beside him again. "If you don't want to go back to school. . . ."

"It would just be a waste," she said.

"And I've really got a future there at Mid-State, I guess."

"If Joe can't hold onto his job, that's his problem," Emma said. "You can't worry about him."

"You know what we could do?" Richie said.

Emma waited expectantly.

"If you got a job," Richie said.

She nodded eagerly.

Richie cleared his throat. "Well, I was just thinking. . . . It makes a lot of sense. And they won't let you buy on time if you're in college, Joe says. So, I might stay on at work. And then, if you got a job, too." He cleared his throat again.

Emma was still nodding.

"What we might do . . . we might get—" He swallowed. "—get together and—"

"Richie, are you going to say it?"

"—and get married."

"Oh, Richie!" she squealed. She threw her arms around him.

From upstairs came the voice: "Emma, did you call me?"

Emma broke away from the kiss and shouted toward the stairs. "No, Mother!"

"I thought I heard you calling me. Who were you calling? Your father?"

"I wasn't calling anybody, Mother," Emma replied drearily.

"Is Richie still there?"

"*Yeeeeeesss,* Mother."

"Isn't it getting late?"

"All right, Mother."

Silence from upstairs.

Emma cuddled up to Richie. "Just think, no more of that," she whispered.

"Yeah, no more of that," Richie replied blissfully, visions of risque dancing in his head.

SIX

"Did anybody see my wallet?" Richie asked, arriving in the kitchen for breakfast.

"Right there on your plate, dear," his mother told him. Marion Cunningham was at the stove, slicing carrots into a stew that the family would have for dinner that evening. "I found it on the stairs. You really should be more careful with it."

"I didn't lose it, Mom," Richie said, seating himself at the table. "I put it on the stairs so I'd find it when I came down this morning."

"Why there?" his father asked. "Why not on your chest."

"I never look on the chest in the morning," Richie replied. "But I always look at the stair steps in the morning. My eyes aren't all the way open, and if I don't look at the steps, I fall."

Howard Cunningham was silent for a second, then, addressing his wife, he said, "I wonder if other families have conversations like this in the morning."

"How do you want your eggs, dear?" Marian asked her son.

"Scrambled."

"Coming up," she replied cheerily.

"Dad, talking about other families," Richie said, "Emma and I are going to get married."

Howard, reading the morning paper, nodded vaguely. Then, a moment later, he slowly raised his eyes from the paper and stared at Richie dubiously, obviously doubting that he had actually heard what he thought he heard. Richie was tucking his wallet into his back pocket. Howard Cunningham then turned his questioning look toward his wife. She was standing at the stove, an egg in each hand, a totally stunned expression on her face. Clearly, Howard decided, his ears had not deceived him—Richie had announced that he and Emma were going to be married. That conclusion was confirmed when he saw Marion emerge slowly from the trance and then break the two eggs that were to have been her son's breakfast into the stew.

Even so, Howard insisted on hearing it once more before he would believe it. "Richie, would you repeat what you just told me?"

"Emma and I are going to get married."

"Someday, you mean?"

"As soon as we can."

"Dear," Marion said, "is there some reason why you have to— That is, I mean, is there some particular reason why you and Emma *want* to get married?" She took in a deep breath, waiting.

Richie turned in the chair, looking at her puzzledly. "The same reason everybody gets married," he replied.

"But no *special* reason?"

"I don't know what you mean."

"That's a relief, at least," Marion said.

"Don't you think you're just a little bit young to be getting married, Richie?" his father said.

"I don't see how you can say that, Dad. It isn't some kid thing. We thought about it and came to a mature decision. It's all worked out."

Marion choked back a sob.

"Won't you feel a little strange, being the only old married couple in high school?" Howard asked Richie.

"We're not going back to school. I'm going to stay on at Mid-State. I've been told that I've got a big future there. And Emma will get a job, too. Maybe at the telephone company. That way, we'll have plenty of money."

Marion's sob escaped.

"Mom, why are you crying?" Richie asked.

"She's happy," his father told him. "Now, about this marriage—when is it supposed to take place?"

"We have to find an apartment," Richie replied. "And buy some furniture."

"How can you afford all that?"

"We'll buy the furniture on time," Richie replied. "And all we need for the apartment is the first month's rent. After that, we'll play it by ear."

Howard nodded. "I was a little worried there for a minute," he said, "but now I can see the maturity behind the decision."

Marion Cunningham put a plate of stew in front of Richie. "Here are your eggs, dear," she said weepily.

"Mom, they've got carrots in them."

"Oh." She took the plate away.

"Richie, do Emma's parents know about this?" Howard Cunningham asked.

"Not yet, probably. We just decided last night. She'll tell them this morning."

"Oh, well . . . ," Howard said, relieved. "If I were

you, then, I wouldn't go apartment-hunting yet," he said. "I doubt that Mrs. Watt will let Emma leave home. She needs everybody she can get to be lamps and chairs."

Richie laughed.

"I didn't mean that as a joke."

"Why wouldn't they let her get married?" Richie asked. "She's a girl."

"Maybe they'll think she's just a little bit too young."

"I told you, Dad, this isn't a kid thing."

Howard nodded. "Yes, I heard that."

Marion put the stew in front of Richie again. She had removed the carrots.

Richie looked at her, then looked at the stew, then turned his eyes to his father.

"I don't know," Howard Cunningham said. "Either she's taking after your Uncle Frank or she's in love."

"Oh, my!" Marion said, finally realizing what she had done. Retrieving the stew, she returned to the stove with it.

Richie took an apple from the bowl in the center of the table. "I've got to go, Mom," he said. He took another apple and a banana. "This'll hold me till lunch," he said, departing.

Marion wainted until she heard the front screen door close, then broke into a flood of tears. "Oh, Howard—what are we going to do?"

"You're already doing it," he said.

"We've got to stop him!"

"Marion, I'm sure Mr. and Mrs. Watt will do that for us," Howard said. "Think, now. Can you imagine them letting Emma quit school and get married? Today, she'll tell them, and that will be the end of that."

"But suppose it isn't?"

"Well . . . in that case . . . we'll get the families together and talk this out sensibly. Don't worry, Marion, it's going to work out all right."

"How can you be so sure?"

"Because Richie is now taking care of his billfold and he knows when he's being served stew instead of scrambled eggs."

"Howard, I—"

"Don't you know what that means?" Howard said confidently. "He's no longer in love."

"But he's *engaged!*"

"That's an improvement, Marion," he insisted. "An engagement is vulnerable. Love isn't."

She stifled the tears. "I just wish I could be as sure as you are," she said.

"You're not alone," he told her. "I wish I could be that sure, too."

At work, Richie kept an eye out for Joe Ferguson, anxious to tell him the news. But the morning passed without Joe making an appearance. At noon, on his lunch hour, Richie went looking for him. He walked up and down the aisles between the stacks of cartons calling his name. There was no response. So Richie began looking into the empty cartons that were sitting around. In one, he found Joe, sound asleep at the bottom of the box.

"Joe!"

Ferguson stirred.

"Joe—it's me!"

Ferguson, on his back, opened one eye and peered up blearily.

"I want to talk to you," Richie told him.

Joe's other eye opened. "Didn't you get the check?" he asked fuzzily.

"What check?"

"For that ten bucks. I put a check in the mail to you."

Richie shook his head. "I didn't get it."

"It's in the mail," Joe told him.

Richie pulled back. Joe Ferguson's breath smelled heavily of beer.

"You'll get it tomorrow," Joe said.

"Yeah, okay. But that's not what I want to talk to you about. Joe, I'm getting married. Me and Emma."

Ferguson stared at him sourly.

"Me and Emma—we're getting married," Richie repeated.

"Did you wake me up to tell me that? I thought you wanted your money."

"No, about me and Emma," Richie said, grinning. "What do you think?"

Joe turned over onto his side. "Go away, will you?"

Surprised and puzzled by the reaction, Richie was silent for a moment. Then he said, "We're going to get an apartment, just like you and Millie. Do you know where there are any places?"

"Try the funny farm," Joe replied.

"What do you mean?"

"You must be nuts."

"Joe, you better come out of there," Richie said. "Mr. Starch is going to be looking for you."

"Go away, Richie."

"You better not let him catch you. He was talking

to me . . . you better watch it, I think he wants to fire you."

"Don't be a dumb kid."

"No kidding, Joe, about that apartment. Is there a place in your building, do you think? I don't even know where to look."

Silence.

"Joe . . . ?"

The sound of snoring.

"Joe!"

Ferguson started, then groaned and looked up at Richie again.

"I have to find out about buying on time," Richie told him. "Will they sell to you on time if you're not married yet? That's the problem, see. If we can't buy the furniture until *after* we get married, then we won't have it when we move into the apartment. I don't want to move in with nothing there—just empty rooms. How do they work that?"

"Richie, if you don't shut up and leave me alone, I'm not going to pay you that ten bucks."

"You said it's already in the mail."

"I'm telling you—"

"Okay, okay."

Richie withdrew and walked up the aisle. As he was leaving, he heard the snoring again—and, at the same time, he saw the supervisor standing at the far end of the aisle, scowling and looking around.

"Where's Ferguson?" Mr. Starch asked, as Richie approached.

"Around," Richie replied. "I just saw him."

"Which way did he go?"

"It's hard to say," Richie replied.

The supervisor stomped off. "When I find that no-good. . . ."

Richie returned to work. He was perplexed by Joe Ferguson's reaction to his announcement that he and Emma were going to be married. The way Joe thought about marriage, Richie had expected glee and congratulations. Had Joe, for some reason, changed his mind? That seemed highly unlikely. The hangover, undoubtedly, was to blame for Joe's grumpy behavior.

As it turned out, the Watts did not object to the proposed marriage. Consequently, a meeting of the families was arranged, to be held at the Cunningham home.

"I don't understand them," Marion said, as she and Howard waited that evening for Mr. and Mrs. Watt and Emma to arrive. "Don't they realize how young Emma is?"

"Maybe they didn't get a birth certificate with her," Howard said.

"I don't understand you, either," Marion complained. "How can you be so calm?"

"I'm not calm, I'm numb."

"I wonder what's wrong with Emma," Marion said.

"What does that mean?"

"Why are her parents so anxious to get rid of her?"

"Marion . . . don't think like that. It will just make it worse. I suspect the Watts did the same thing we did—they didn't raise any objections because they thought the whole thing would fall through. They probably thought we would say no to Richie and take the problem off their hands—just as we thought they would say no to Emma. It's a misunderstanding, that's all."

"Maybe it isn't," she said. "What do we do in that case?"

"Well. . . ."

"Say no, that's what we'll do," Marian said.

Howard shook his head. "That would only make Richie and Emma more determined than ever. Marion, they're young, yes, but they're not infants. They're entitled to reasons."

"We'll give them the reasons and we'll say no."

"What reasons?"

"They're too young."

"Other people have gotten married at their age. And, for some of them, it's worked out fine."

"Howard! You're not going along with this, are you?"

"Marion . . . I've been thinking. . . . Suppose Richie and Emma *are* in love? Suppose they *are* ready to get married? That's possible, you know."

"I *know* my own son," Marion replied sharply. "He is *not* ready to get married."

"That's one of the problems, Marion—he *is* our son. But what if he was a stranger? Would you still be so sure that he was too young? He has a job, you know. He goes to work every day. That indicates a certain amount of responsibility, doesn't it? Wouldn't you say, maybe, that he's a sensible kid . . . sensible enough to know what he wants?"

"Richie isn't a stranger."

"All right. What will we do, though, if we say no and Richie and Emma get married anyway?"

"Richie wouldn't—"

"Wouldn't he? He thinks he's made a mature decision. He doesn't think he's too young. Telling him he's too young won't change his mind about it. He has to find out for himself."

"But it will be too late—he'll be married."

"They're not going out and get married tomorrow. There'll be some time." He smiled confidently. "Anyway," he said, "I'm pretty sure that by the time this little get-together ends the marriage plans will be off. I doubt that the Watts are any more anxious to have another son than we are to have another daughter. As I said—it's just a misunderstanding."

There was a knock at the door.

"That's them," Howard said, rising. "I'll answer the door, you get Richie."

They went into the entryway and Howard stopped at the door to welcome the Watt family, while Marion headed up the stairs to summon Richie, who was in his room.

"Lovely," Mrs. Watt said, entering the living room, accompanied by her husband and Emma and Howard Cunningham. "That lamp is just perfect," she said, pointing. "But have you tried it on the other side of the chair?"

"Don't start arranging," her husband said. To Howard, he said, "Well, big day, isn't it?"

"Oh, I don't know," Howard replied. "We've had that lamp on the other side of the chair. It looked about the same."

Mr. Watt laughed.

"Have you considered a shorter lamp, then?" Mrs. Watt said.

"No, but we once played with the idea of a higher chair." Mrs. Watt brightened, as if the notion of a higher chair were an important breakthrough.

"You'll learn that you have to watch what you say to her, Howard," Mr. Watt said. "No sense of humor." He beamed. "But, we'll be seeing a lot of each other from now on," he said. "You'll catch on."

Richie and his mother arrived. Hellos were said. Then they all found seats and the meeting, informally, came to order.

"You were probably as surprised as we were when this came out," Howard Cunningham said to Mr. and Mrs. Watt.

"No, not really," Mrs. Watt replied. "Richie and Emma didn't do much talking when they were downstairs alone, so I thought they must be up to something."

"Oh. Well, we didn't have that advantage, so we were surprised," Howard said. "Although I suppose the fact that Richie kept his billfold in the oven should have been a clue." He glanced at Marion, then, addressing the Watts again, said, "What I was getting at is, now that you've had time to think it over, you're probably wondering if the kids are *really* old enough."

Mr. Watts shook his head. "Hadn't entered my mind," he said.

"Dad, I told you this isn't a kid thing," Richie said.

"We've thought it all through," Emma said.

"I'm proud of them," Mrs. Watt said. "They decided all by themselves. When I was their age, I didn't dare have one thought without first getting permission."

"Those were the good old days," Mr. Watt said.

"Maybe we ought to go over the details, though, just for the heck of it," Howard said. He spoke directly to Richie and Emma. "There just might be something you haven't thought of," he said.

"The apartment and the furniture," Richie said. "What else is there?"

"Richie, you've been a member of a family for a while now," his mother said. "Haven't you noticed that there's something besides just the man and the woman?"

"Oh, sure. But we don't need a car right away."

"Listen," Mr. Watt said, frowning, addressing Howard. "You and Marion aren't against this, are you? I asked Richie how you took it and he said fine."

"As a matter of fact—" Marion began.

"What she means is," Howard said, breaking in, "we want to be sure that everybody—not just Richie and Emma—has thought it through. For instance, you might be thinking—in the back of your mind—that Emma is still a little young to be getting married."

"She's the same age as Richie," Mrs. Watt pointed out.

"Girls are younger than boys," Marion said.

The others peered at her.

"For their age, I mean," Marion explained.

"Look, let's put our cards on the table," Mr. Watt said. "Here's the way I see it. Emma's a girl. What's a girl for? To get married. To be somebody's wife. So, why wait?"

"What he means is," Mrs. Watt said, "Richie is such a nice boy. I'm sure Emma won't ever find anyone any nicer."

A sound came from Emma. She had started to speak, then had fallen silent again.

"What is it, dear?" her mother asked.

"Nothing," she said, looking away.

"Anyway, as I say, that's how we see it," Emma's father said to Howard. "But, if you have some other idea . . . If you think Emma's not good enough for your boy, or—"

"No," Howard broke in. "We both like Emma very much."

Mr. Watt broke into a wide smile. "That settles it, I guess."

"It will be a beautiful wedding," Mrs. Watt said dreamily.

"After you rearrange the flowers, it will be," her husband said.

"The furniture. . . ." Emma said.

Her father nodded. "Right." He spoke to Howard again. "Richie and Emma are a little worried about getting credit," he said. "I thought I'd advance them the cash for the down payment on the furniture. But if you'd rather do that. . . . I don't want to horn in where it's not my place."

"No, go ahead, horn," Howard said. "I don't know how good an idea it is to start off in debt. . . ."

"Don't worry about that. They'll clean up at the wedding." Mr. Watt leaned forward. "How are your relatives fixed?" he asked. He raised a hand to keep back a possibly negative response. "Don't think I'm being nosy. I was just thinking, if they kick in big, Richie and Emma might be able to start out with a car, too, besides the furniture. I try to look on the rosy side."

"How does this sound—an all-white wedding?" Mrs. Watt said.

"Brides always wear white," her husband said. "What other kind of wedding is there?"

"I mean everybody in white—the groom, too," Mrs. Watt explained. "And the ushers—everybody."

"I don't know, that sounds a little sacreligious to me," Mr. Watt said. "This isn't a circus, this is a wedding."

"What about the children!" Marion said suddenly. Obviously, she had held back as long as she could.

"Oh, yes, the little flower girls in white, too," Mrs. Watt replied.

"I'm talking about *children,*" Marion said. "I'm talking about Richie and Emma and *children.*"

"Babies, she means," Howard said.

Mr. Watt's facial muscles tightened. "I don't think we ought to talk about things like that in front of the kids," he said. "I don't discuss that subject in my own house and I wouldn't want to do it in your house, either." He spoke to Howard. "You and I and your wife and my wife can get together separately and hash that out," he said. "But let's not rake it over the coals in mixed company."

"Well, maybe there's nothing to worry about," Howard said. "If Emma doesn't know about babies by now, there's always the outside chance that she'll never learn."

Mr. Watt, red-faced, stuck a finger inside his collar to loosen it.

"At the reception," Mrs. Watt said, "I see a centerpiece of white carnations—in the shape of angels."

Mr. Watt shook his head in dismay. "Flying carnations. You really do want to turn this into a circus."

"Who's paying for all this?" Richie asked.

"Now, there's a boy with his head on his shoulders," Mr. Watt said. "The bride's parents do the paying," he told Richie.

Richie relaxed. "Oh. I was thinking—"

"Dear," Mrs. Watt said to her husband, "It's got to be a big wedding. We didn't have a big wedding and I've always wanted one."

"We'll talk about it at home," he answered.

"There go the angels," Howard Cunningham said.

Mr. Watt rose. "I guess we've covered everything," he said.

"Marion, we'll get together tomorrow and start planning the wedding," Mrs. Watt said, getting up. "I have oodles of ideas. I've been saving them up from when we had such a little dinky wedding."

"Just don't go hog wild," Mr. Watt said.

"Incidentally, when is this wedding?" Howard asked.

There was silence.

"Well, there *is* an awful, awful lot to do," Mrs. Watt said.

"I don't know . . ." Emma said. "What do you think, Richie?"

He shrugged. "Any time, I guess."

"I'll make up a schedule," Mrs. Watt said. "We'll see how much time we need for the important things, then, at the end, we'll have the wedding. It's the only sensible way."

"Fine with me," her husband said.

"Great idea," Howard said happily.

The Watts departed.

Marion looked at her son and tears came to her eyes.

"Jiminy, Mom," Richie said, embarrassed. He headed for his room.

Marion turned to Howard. "It's all over . . . we've lost him," she said, weeping.

"Marion, relax—there won't be a wedding," Howard said.

She stared at him puzzledly. "How do you know that?"

"Because Mrs. Watt is in charge of it," he said. "How long have they been married? Twenty years? And she still hasn't got her living room arranged. By the time she gets that wedding set, Richie and Emma will be in the old folks' home."

SEVEN

"Why does your mother keep telling me I'd look taller in white?" Richie said to Emma a few Sundays later when they were aboard the bus that would take them to the beach. "I thought your father turned thumbs down on that all-white wedding idea."

"She won't give up," Emma replied wearily. "My father even called in our pastor, but he couldn't talk her out of it either. I think he sort of got to like the idea too."

"I'd feel like a nut," Richie said.

"Why?"

"Girls wear white, guys don't."

"You know why, don't you?" Emma said.

"Sure. That's the way it is."

"I mean the reason."

"Girls look good in white."

"No. It's because girls are supposed to be virgins. But boys, they can be anything they want." She looked out the bus window. "It's not really fair, you know."

Richie shrugged. It seemed fair to him. But it wasn't important enough to argue about.

"Do you think your friends will be at the beach?" Emma asked.

"Where else?"

"At last, I'm finally going to meet them." She looked toward him. "Do they know about us?"

"They must by now," Richie replied. "I told Potsie a couple days ago."

"I thought we were going to keep it a secret until we got a ring and everything."

"I told him it was a secret—that's why I'm sure they all know by now."

Emma laughed. "I bet you're right. Won't you feel kind of funny?" she said.

"How?"

"Well, it's different. You're practically married and they're still kids."

"I'm still the same guy—except more mature," Richie said.

"Do you think they'll like me?" Emma asked.

"Why not?"

"Well, the girls— I mean, I just moved to town and here we are, you and me, getting married. They might be jealous." She looked at him narrowly. "Did you have a girl?"

"Nobody special."

"Why not?" she asked, looking at him as if he might have some flaw that she had not discovered before.

"I liked to play the field," Richie explained.

That seemed to satisfy her. She looked out the bus window again.

"Did you have a guy where you used to live?" Richie asked.

"Huh-uh . . . not really."

He looked at her in the same way that, a moment

before, she she had looked at him. "How come?" he asked.

For a second, Emma did not respond. Then, facing him again, she looked at him deliberately and said, "I liked to play the field."

Richie's expression became taut—then he grinned. "You're kidding."

"You did," she said. "You just told me so."

"Yeah, I know, but— You were kidding, though, weren't you?"

"Maybe." She turned toward the window once more.

"Sure you were," Richie said.

No more was said for a while. Emma continued to face the window. Every few moments, she sighed.

"Something the matter?" Richie asked finally.

"No."

"Are you okay?"

"I guess." She sighed again. "Did you hear what my father said?"

"About the angels?"

"No, about me. He said I'm a girl and what's a girl for? To get married and be a wife."

Richie nodded. "Oh, yeah, I remember that."

"I didn't know he thought about me that way."

"Why not? He's your father."

"No, what I mean is, what he was saying was, there's nothing else I'm any good for."

"He didn't say that,"

"That's what he meant. The way he sees me, I don't have any choice, I can get married or . . . or I can dry up and blow away or something."

"He didn't say *anything* like that," Richie protested.

"What did he mean then?"

"All he meant was, you're a girl and you're supposed to get married."

"Suppose I didn't want to?"

"Everybody *wants* to."

"But suppose I *didn't?*"

Richie shrugged. "You'd be an old maid."

"In other words, I can get married or I can be an old maid?"

"What else is there?" Richie asked, perplexed.

"Don't talk to me!" Emma said angrily.

"Hey—what'd I do?"

Silence.

Richie puzzled. What was bothering her all of a sudden? What was she all steamed up about? Because he'd said she was a girl and she was supposed to get married? What was wrong with that? She *was* a girl, she *was* supposed to get married. That didn't mean she wasn't good for anything. She was good for getting married and being a wife.

Then a possible explanation occurred to him. Maybe she was having female trouble. He wasn't sure what that was. But, clearly, it was a trouble and it affected females. And Emma was a female. How to handle it, though? By doing what his father did when his mother started banging pans in the kitchen, probably.

"Whatever I did, I'm sorry," he said.

"You didn't do anything."

It was working out. "If you don't want to go to the beach, we don't have to," he said. "We can stay on the bus and go on back."

"No, I want to meet your friends."

"Whatever you want," he said.

She turned to him. Her eyes were moist. "I wasn't

mad at you," she said, trying to smile. "I just— I don't know."

His diagnosis had apparently been correct—female trouble. Otherwise, she would have been able to explain it. Females probably didn't like to talk about their trouble—whatever it was.

"Look, if you want me to wear white at the wedding . . . well, okay," Richie said. "I'll feel funny, though."

Emma laughed.

"What'd I say?"

"Nothing." But she continued to laugh.

Richie dropped the subject, glad to be done with it.

At the beach, Richie and Emma got Cokes, then set off across the sand.

"Everybody's probably down by the lifeguard," Richie said.

"Everybody's right here," Emma replied, looking around at the crowded beach.

"The guys, I mean. That's where we always meet, by the lifeguard."

"The girls, too?"

"Everybody."

They came to the girls first. Richie introduced Emma to Sally and Marlene and Betty and Alice and Susie and Louise and Mary Lou. Each girl responded with a hi, while examining Emma speculatively. They were amiable but disinterested—or so it seemed to Richie.

"I'm going over and see the guys," Richie told Emma.

"All right."

Richie left. After he had gone a few paces he began

to feel concern about the indifferent reception that Emma had received from the girls. But when he glanced back, that feeling quickly passed. The other girls had closed in around Emma and were firing questions at her from all directions.

The guys greeted him casually—just as if he had been around all summer.

"Is that her?" Jack asked, nodding in the direction of the girls.

"Uh-huh," Richie replied, joining them.

"I hear you're getting married," Tom said.

"Who told you that?"

"Are you?"

"Who told you?"

"I didn't tell him," Potsie said.

"Did Potsie tell you?" Richie asked Tom.

"I'm not telling. Are you or aren't you?"

"Who told you, that's all I want to know," Richie said.

"I didn't tell him," Potsie said again.

"I bet you're not," Tom said to Richie.

"What do you want to bet?"

"Are you?"

"You said you wanted to bet," Richie countered. "Put your money where your mouth is."

"Yeah, but are you?" Tom asked.

"Sure," Richie said.

The guys looked toward the girls. There was meditative silence as they studied Emma thoroughly. Then Mitch picked up the football that was lying nearby on the sand and began spiraling it into the air and catching it. Ralph made the next move. He got up and went galloping toward the water, then plunged into the surf.

"Somebody go out for a pass," Mitch said.

Gerald rose and ran backwards, going toward the girls.

Mitch put the ball into the air. It wobbled, then skipped off Gerald's fingertips and landed a few inches from the girls and rolled toward them. Alice quickly scooped it up. Gerald walked over to where the girls were seated. A conversation began, highlighted by occasional bursts of laughter.

"Come on!" Mitch called to Gerald.

There was no response.

"I guess I have to go get him," Mitch said, trudging off.

Meanwhile, Ralph had emerged from the water. He discovered to his considerable surprise that he had come ashore near where the girls were gathered. Politeness demanded that he stop by and assist Mitch and Gerald in retrieving the football.

"Boy, you don't let any grass grow under your feet, do you?" Potsie said to Richie.

"When you're ready, you're ready," Richie replied. "Did you tell Tom?"

"I didn't tell him, honest." He turned to Tom. "Did I tell you?"

Tom ignored the question. "Are you engaged?" he asked Richie.

"The same as."

"Did you get her a ring?"

"We're still looking," Richie told him.

Mitch returned.

"Where's my football?" Tom asked.

"They've got it."

"I better get it," Tom said, getting up.

"I'll help you!" Jack said, jumping to his feet.

As they were leaving, Gerald and Ralph came back.

"Nice," Gerald said to Richie.

Richie shrugged. "Yeah, she's pretty nice."

"What's it like?" Ralph asked him.

"What's what like?"

"You know."

Richie shrugged again.

"There goes the ball," Potsie said.

The others looked. Susie was running toward the water, yelping, with Tom racing after her.

Potsie got up. He, too, ran toward the water.

"I thought Tom was going with Sally," Richie said, as Tom, having chased Susie into the surf, tried—but not too hard—to wrestle the football from her.

"Not any more," Mitch said.

"You didn't tell Ralph what it's like," Gerald said to Richie.

"What what's like?"

"Like he said—you know."

Mitch answered the question. "It's just like going steady," he told Gerald.

Gerald looked to Richie for confirmation.

"Like going steady . . . and then some," Richie said.

Eyes lit up.

"When you're just as good as engaged, your life is your own," Richie told them. "Everybody knows you're going to get married, so they don't bother you."

His friends thought about that for a moment.

"You mean you can do *anything?*" Mitch said.

"Why not?"

"Sure, you're as good as married anyway," Gerald said.

Tom and Potsie were now carrying Susie from the water, one holding her by the wrists, the other holding her by the ankles. The football had already been thrown up onto the beach. Susie was shrieking, pretending outrage.

"I once knew a guy that practiced free love," Mitch said.

"By himself?" Gerald asked.

"No, you know what I mean."

The others, having had a close look at Emma, began returning.

"I think Susie goes for me," Jack said.

"I know she does," Potsie told him. "Did you hear what Marlene said to her? She said it was the first time Susie'd got her bathing suit wet since she bought it."

"Wow!" Jack said, grinning. "I didn't hear it. How'd she say it?"

"You know—like girls do."

"What'll I do now?" Jack said. "I can't handle two of them."

"Who's that guy over there?" Richie asked, looking toward the girls. A tall, muscular young man with a blond crewcut was standing at the edge of the circle of girls, talking with them. He was getting their rapt and appreciative attention.

"That's Bobby Scull—remember him?" Potsie said.

"Is that Bobby Scull?" Richie replied. "Wasn't he fat?"

"He's not now," Potsie said. "He played football at college last year. That's good for a freshman."

"It's a little college," Mitch said. "Anybody can make the team."

"What's he doing talking to the girls?" Richie said.

"He's a morning lifeguard," Mitch said.

"Isn't he kind of old?"

"They like that," Potsie said. "It's a big thrill."

"He wouldn't give any of them a tumble," Gerald said.

"You worried, Rich?" Tom asked, grinning.

Richie faced his friends. "Why would I worry? We're as good as engaged."

"Let's go duck Betty," Mitch said to Gerald. "Boy, can she scream."

Mitch and Gerald leaped up and ran toward the girls.

"I think I'll go see what's doing, too," Richie said, rising more slowly.

"What're you worried about, Richie?" Tom said, grinning widely.

"Who's worried?"

"Then what're you going over for?"

"Can't I just go over?"

"You must be worried."

"I don't have to be worried just because I'm going over."

"Lay off," Potsie said to Tom.

"All I asked him was what he's worried about."

"Why don't you just lay off?" Potsie said.

Tom directed another question at Richie. "If you're not worried—"

But by then, Richie had escaped.

Howard Cunningham raised his eyes from the newspaper as he heard footfalls on the front porch. A few moments later, Richie appeared in the entryway and looked into the living room. He had a confusing expression on his face. He looked mildly dazed—and happy about it.

"Dad . . . is that you?" Richie said.

"It was the last time I checked," Howard replied. "Have I changed?"

"I think the sun affected my eyes," Richie told him, entering the living room. "I'm not used to it." He sank into a chair and slumped.

"Isn't it just possible that you're tired?" Howard Cunningham said. "You've been at the beach almost all day."

"I can take it," Richie said. He seemed to want to smile broadly, but he could manage only about half of it.

"You look pleased," Howard said. "Or, at least, you look as if you'd *like* to look pleased—if you could just stay awake."

"Is it late?"

"Everybody else is in bed. Your sister was the last to turn in. She just went up." He looked at Richie closely. "Maybe you ought to call it a day, too," he said. "It's back to work tomorrow."

The other half of the broad smile appeared on Richie's face.

"Don't you think you ought to go to bed?" his father said. "It's back to work tomorrow."

Richie nodded. But he remained seated.

"Did something spectacular happen today, Richie?"

"No."

"Well—"

"There was this guy Bobby Scull out at the beach," Richie said.

"Oh?"

"He goes to college. He's on the football team. But it's only a little college. He's a freshman."

Howard nodded, waiting for the rest of it.

"And he's a lifeguard."

"It's pretty spectacular so far," Howard said.

"He was hanging around Emma all afternoon."

"Oh. . . ."

"When we got ready to go, he wanted to drive us back in his car," Richie said. "It's not his car, it's his dad's car. Emma wanted to."

"Wanted to drive back in the car?"

"Yeah. Only, I said no, we'd come back in the bus, the way we got there."

Howard smiled noncommittally.

"The other guys were coming back on the bus," Richie explained.

"That's a good reason."

"And if you take the bus someplace, you ought to take the bus back."

"Yes, I see—it's a matter of principle."

"Huh?"

"You felt that, having taken the bus to the beach, you had a moral and ethical obligation to take the bus back from the beach," Howard said. "I understand that. That's the kind of straight thinking that's made us great, as a nation and as a people."

"I don't know about that," Richie said. "But Emma still wanted to come back in Bobby Scull's car—his dad's car. It's not his car."

"You probably put your foot down," Howard said.

Richie nodded. "Somebody has to wear the pants in the family," he said.

"So you came back by bus."

The whole smile came out this time, wide and bright.

"You won the battle," Howard said.

Richie nodded again.

"The rest of that saying about winning the battle is: and lost the war," Howard said.

"What?"

"Never mind, Richie. Don't you think you ought to go to bed now?"

"I'm not tired," Richie said, pushing himself up a bit in the chair. "I just got too much sun. What's in the paper?"

"Oh . . . about three-quarters ads and one quarter news."

"Anything I ought to know?"

"Well, let's see . . ." Howard said, raising the newspaper. "Here's something that might interest you, since you're leaving school and going out into the business world. It's a story about some new machines—thinking machines. They're called computers. They do mathematics—only a lot faster than humans can."

"What's the hurry?" Richie asked.

"It doesn't say."

"Then who needs them?"

"Well . . . there's an example here. It says that one computer did a job in a little over a hundred hours that it would have taken a man a hundred years to do."

"A math problem?"

"Something like that."

"How do they know the machine was right?" Richie asked.

His father lowered the paper again. "I don't know," he replied, frowning.

"Wouldn't a man have to do it, too, to check it?"

Richie said. "Otherwise, they'd have to take the machine's word for it. And if a man has to do it, too, to check it, what are they saving?"

"Evidently they trust the machine."

"Not me," Richie said. "It's probably just one of those things. You know, they're always coming out with things. But then you never hear about them again. I bet it'll be the same thing with computers. You'll never hear about it again."

"I don't know . . . that's what I thought when they said they could throw pictures through the air."

"That's what I mean," Richie said. "Nobody's ever done it, have they?"

"Television, Richie."

"Oh."

"Richie, your eyes are closing."

"Is that all there is in the paper?"

"Yes. Goodnight, Richie."

With effort, Richie pushed himself up out of the chair. He stood for a moment.

"Are you falling asleep on your feet?"

"I was just thinking," Richie said. "If I don't want to wear white at the wedding, why should I? Except that I sort of half-promised Emma that I would."

"Did she ask you to?"

"No. Not exactly."

"I don't understand, then. Why did you tell her you would?"

"She was mad at me about something. I don't know what. So I told her I'd wear white if she wanted me to. She didn't say what she wanted, though. She laughed. Does that make sense to you?"

"I don't know the details, Richie."

"I don't either," Richie said. "But I think the way to get out of it is the same way I made her ride back on the bus. I'll put my foot down."

"I wouldn't overdo that," Howard advised.

"Somebody has to wear the pants in the family."

"Richie, if you're going to wear the pants in the family, you ought to wear them all the time—not just when you want to break a promise."

"You know, it's not easy just being as good as engaged," Richie said. "Is it easier when you're married?"

"Well, look at it this way," Howard replied. "You've heard the saying that marriage is a partnership, I suppose. That's very true, in a way. But, on the other hand, there comes a time when a decision has to be made and you can't agree on what it should be. In a case like that—" Richie's eyes had become completely glazed over. "Richie . . . ?"

No answer.

Howard Cunningham put the paper aside and got up and waved a hand in front of his son's face. There was no response. Gently, he put his hands on Richie's shoulders and turned him and guided him toward the stairs. The momentum carried Richie forward. He reached the entryway, then moved on up the steps, sound asleep.

EIGHT

Richie lifted a carton of canned turnip greens from the hand cart and raised it to his shoulder. At that same moment, he saw Joe Ferguson coming down the aisle. Joe was weaving. He was also muttering. With the heavy carton still on his shoulder, Richie stood staring at him. His face was contorted in a look of anger and resentment.

"Are you just getting here?" Richie asked, as Joe neared him. "You better keep out of sight. Don't let Mr. Starch see you."

"Nobody pulls that stuff on Joe Ferguson," Joe said sullenly. He halted, wavering. "Listen, Richie, nobody pulls that on Joe. You understand?"

Richie nodded. "Pulls what?" he asked.

"Nobody—but *nobody*. Check?"

"Pulls what?" Richie repeated.

"I wasn't born yesterday," Joe told him. "Anybody that thinks Joe Ferguson was born yesterday better think again."

Richie started toward the stack with the heavy carton, but Joe caught his arm, stopping him.

"Will you let me put this down?" Richie said.

"You know what that dame's done, Richie?"

"Who? Millie?"

"I don't ever want to hear that name again," Joe said belligerently. "Don't ever use that name again in front of me, Richie."

"What'll I call her?"

"I'll tell you what you can call her. Call her no-name, that's what you can call her. As far as I'm concerned, she's nobody any more. Understand?"

Richie started toward the stack again, and once more Joe delayed him.

"She can't pull that stuff on me," Joe said.

"What'd she do?"

"I'll tell you what she did," Joe replied, muttering again. "You want to know what she did? I'll tell you. She got herself pregnant. Can you feature that? Pregnant. You think I'm kidding, don't you? You don't think she could be that dumb. Well, listen, I'm not kidding. She's pregnant. Can you feature that, Richie? You know Millie—did you have any idea that she's that dumb?"

"I don't know. . . . What's—"

"Yeah, you didn't know she was that dumb, either. She had us all fooled," Joe said. "Well, listen, that's not all. You think getting pregnant is dumb? Listen to this. She quit her job."

"Well, maybe—"

"That's what I told her," Joe said, outraged. "First, I said, you get yourself pregnant, and now you quit your job. Who do you think you are, anyway? The Queen of Sheba?" He wavered again and caught hold of Richie for support, nearly taking them both down. "I really told her off," he said, regaining his balance. "Who do you think you are, the Queen of Sheba? That put her in her place."

"Joe, I've got a hole in my shoulder from this carton," Richie complained. Joe was still holding onto him. "Will you let go and let me put it down?"

"You want to know what else she's doing?" Joe said, still clutching Richie.

"I'd rather put this down before I don't have any shoulder left."

"She's laying around the apartment," Joe told him. "She quit her job and she's just laying around. Being sick. Moaning and saying how sick she is. Who wants to listen to that?"

"Joe, you better get out of sight before Mr. Starch sees you," Richie warned.

"That's no fun, Richie, some dame laying around being sick. Where's the laughs? I didn't get married to listen to some dame moan around all over the place. I'm not going to take it. I don't have to take it. I'm no sucker."

"What do you mean?" Richie asked, concerned.

"I'll tell you what I mean. I mean what I say and I say what I mean, that's what I mean. I'm no sucker. I don't have to take that. She double-crossed me, Richie."

A disturbing thought suddenly occurred to Richie. "You don't mean she— I mean, she didn't— It's your . . . I mean, it's your baby, too, isn't it?"

Joe peered at him fuzzily. "What baby?"

"The baby she's pregnant with."

"Ohhhh . . . It's not my kid."

"Oh, boy! You mean she's been stepping out on you?"

Joe looked even more confused. "Who told you that? Why would she do that? I'd knock her block off. What gave you that idea?"

"You said it's not your baby."

"Yeah, it's not. But not in that way. What I mean is, I don't want any kid. She's not going to stick me with any kid. I'm no sucker. Kids are no fun, Richie." Tears came to his eyes. "It's a real crime. We really had it great. And now she's done this."

"You better get out of here, Joe," Richie said. "If Mr. Starch sees you, it'll even be worse. Why don't you go home?"

"That dame's there. You think I want to see that, her being sick. Did I tell you, Richie? She quit her job?"

"Go find a box, then," Richie said. "Sleep it off. You'll feel different."

"I could use a beer," Joe said. He released Richie and looked back along the aisle. "Is the coast clear?"

"Don't go that way. Mr. Starch might see you. Find a box."

"No, I got to get a beer." He started off, wobbling. "You just remember: I'm no sucker," he said mushily. "Nobody pulls the wool over my eyes."

"Take it easy, Joe."

"I wasn't born yesterday," Joe said, moving on. He bounced off one wall of cartons, staggered across the aisle and hit the other wall, then wobbled on, muttering again.

Richie slid the carton from his aching shoulder, putting it on the stack. When he looked again, Joe had reached the end of the aisle. A moment later, he was gone.

Richie resumed work, depressed. He was stunned by

the speed with which Joe's and Millie's supposedly perfect marriage had evidently collapsed. Where had all the happiness gone? But perhaps Joe hadn't really meant all the things he had said. Maybe it was the booze talking—as the saying went. That was probably it. When Joe sobered up, he'd see things differently. He'd be happy about the baby. Or, at least, he'd accept it and get used to the idea. After all, Millie wasn't all to blame. She hadn't gotten pregnant alone.

It would work out, Richie told himself. But he didn't believe it.

When Richie arrived at the Watt house that evening, he was met by Mrs. Watt.

"I'm glad you're here, dear," she said. "We've got to talk about the wedding. There are so many things to do, and, of course, I can't make a move until I get yours and Emma's approval. After all, it's your wedding, isn't it?"

"Where is she?" Richie asked, looking toward the stairs.

"No, she's not up there. I sent her to the store—" She frowned. "That was almost an hour ago," she said. "I wonder what's keeping her? Well, she probably met someone. You know how girls go on when they get together. I'm just glad I didn't ask her to get anything that would spoil."

"She's been gone a whole hour?" Richie said.

"Well, something like that. Make yourself comfortable, dear," she said, gesturing toward the living room. "But, remember, when Emma comes back, we've got to talk. Weddings don't plan themselves." She scurried off in the direction of the kitchen.

Richie went into the living room and sat down on the sofa.

A few moments later, Bobs appeared in the doorway. He was holding a large, scruffy-looking ceramic elephant.

"What do you think I can get for this?" Bobs asked.

"Why would anybody want it?"

"It would make a good lamp," Bobs said. "Somebody could put a wire in it and put a shade on it. That's what makes stuff valuable."

"It looks like somebody's throw-out to me," Richie said.

"It is. It was broke in two when I found it. I glued it together. Think I could get a dollar for it?"

"Not from me," Richie said.

"You're going to need a lamp when you get married," Bobs said. "You couldn't get a lamp for a dollar."

"That's not a lamp."

"It's as good as. All it needs is some wire and a shade. I can get you the wire. Fifty cents. And, if you just wait, I'll have a shade one of these days."

"We'll probably get a new lamp," Richie told him.

"Where're you going to get a new lamp made out of an elephant?"

"Someplace. Anyway, what do we want with an elephant lamp?"

"How about seventy-five cents?" Bobs asked.

"I don't want it."

Bobs shrugged. "Okay. If I can't sell it, I'll save it and give it to you as a wedding present."

"For how much?" Richie asked.

"Free."

"I'll give you two bits not to," Richie said.

Bobs considered. "If I can't sell it to somebody, it's a deal," he said. He moved on, going up the stairs.

Richie rose and went to the windows and looked out, wondering what was delaying Emma. How long could it take to go to the store, anyway? The store was only about four blocks away. Maybe he ought to walk that way and meet her. But if she was with some girl, gabbing, he didn't want to get mixed up in that. Girls' conversations drove him crazy.

He went back to the sofa.

Mr. Watt appeared in the doorway. He glanced in the direction of the kitchen, then entered the living room and sat down in the chair that faced the sofa.

"Richie, I'm depending on you to hold the line on this wedding," he said, keeping his voice low. "You know how my wife is. But don't let her buffalo you."

"On what?" Richie asked.

"She's talking about everybody in white now," Mr. Watt told him. "Not just you and Emma. Me and your folks, too. Your dad wouldn't hold still for that, would he?"

"I don't know."

"You put your foot down and he won't have to," Mr. Watt said. "We've got to stick together on this. You don't want to look like a sissy, do you?"

Richie shook his head.

"Your friends will be there. You don't want them to see you in a white monkey suit. Just tell her it's out. And tell her not to go hog wild on the reception, either. You don't want her to hire a hall, do you? We can have it right here at the house. We can put up some card tables and hang up some crepe and some Japanese lanterns and it'll look fine. How does that sound to you?"

"Fine, I guess."

"You tell her that," Mr. Watt said. "Don't tell her it was my idea, though. This is man to man—okay?"

"Sure," Richie said.

"Don't let her buffalo you, old man." He rose and winked, then left, going toward the back of the house.

Richie got up and went to the window again. A few minutes later, a car stopped in front of the house. Emma was in the passenger's seat. Richie could not see the driver. He guessed that one of the neighbors had seen her walking home from the store and had offered her a ride.

Emma was still in the car. What could she have to talk about to a neighbor about that was so important? The wedding probably. Or the price of groceries. Take any subject, and two women could sit and talk about it for hours. But Emma wasn't a woman yet—she was still a girl. He hoped that getting married wasn't going to change her *that* much.

Then the driver got out of the car. Richie was stunned. It wasn't a neighbor, it was Bobby Scull. He circled the rear of the car, then opened the door on the passenger's side. Emma got out, holding a grocery bag. She stood talking to Scull. He had a cocky grin on his face. Now, Emma and Scull laughed. What was so funny? What were they talking about? How long had they been together, anyway?

At last, Emma started toward the house. Quickly, Richie returned to the sofa. He heard Emma opening the front door. Then she appeared in the entryway.

"Oh, hi," she said.

"Is that all you got, just one bag?" Richie said tightly. "I thought you bought out the whole store—you've been gone long enough."

She looked at him narrowly, then said, "I've got to take this stuff back to the kitchen," and moved on.

Waiting, Richie fumed. It wasn't enough that she was out riding around with Bobby Scull, she'd had him drive her right up to the door, where everybody could see her get out of his car. They both knew what that made Richie look like. That was probably what they were laughing about. Big joke.

Emma returned. "My mother's coming in," she said, sitting down in the chair. "She's finishing the dishes."

Richie remained silent, tight-lipped.

"What's the matter?" Emma asked.

"I saw you in that car," he told her.

"Are you mad about *that?*"

"I'm not mad. What were you doing with *him,* that's all I want to know."

"What do you mean, what was I doing? What do you think I was doing?"

"I don't know. You were sure gone a long time, that's all I know."

"We went for a ride, that's all," Emma said.

"You were supposed to be at the store."

"I was. When I came out, Bobby was there. He asked me if I wanted a ride home, so I said yes. But then we got talking and we just rode around."

"Talking about what?"

"College. He was telling me how it is. It's a lot of fun. Do you know he only has classes three days a week? And then not all day, either. For instance, on Tuesdays, he only has two classes. Both in the morning. So he has the whole rest of the day off. Wouldn't that be great?"

"I thought you didn't care if you went to college."

"I don't, I guess," she said. "I was just telling you what we were talking about—you're so suspicious."

"Who's suspicious? It looks funny, that's all," Richie said. "You must've been gone almost two hours. He could tell you everything there is to say about college in five minutes."

"What do you mean by that?"

"Nothing. But what were you doing all that time, just riding? Didn't you even stop once?"

"We stopped a *lot* of times," Emma said sharply.

"Yeah, that's what I guessed."

"At every stop light," Emma told him.

"And that's all?"

"Richie, you sound like you own me," Emma complained.

"We're as good as engaged, aren't we?"

"That doesn't mean you *own* me."

"It doesn't mean you're supposed to jump in somebody's car every time he comes along, either," Richie countered. "Even though that isn't his car—it's his dad's."

"Now what do you mean by that?"

"He's not so hot," Richie said. "That's just a *little* college he goes to, you know. He probably couldn't even get in a *big* college."

"And maybe you couldn't get in *any* college," Emma said cuttingly. "Maybe *that's* why you decided not to go—because you knew you couldn't!"

"I could."

"That's what *you* say."

They heard Mrs. Watt approaching.

Emma looked toward the windows and Richie fixed his gaze on his hands.

"Here we are!" Mrs. Watt said breezily, entering the room. "Oh, do we have things to talk about! So much to get settled." She sat down in the other chair. "First," she said, "I've talked to the people at the American Legion hall and it's free for the second Saturday in August. So, we'll build around that. Is that all right with you, Richie?"

"I don't care. But I was thinking, maybe—" He gestured, indicating the living room. "—If we put up some card tables—"

"Just forget what Mr. Watt says," Mrs. Watt interrupted. "If he had his way, we'd have the reception in the kitchen and serve leftovers." She addressed her daughter. "Emma, pay attention."

"I'm listening," Emma said, still facing toward the windows.

"Now, about white," Mrs. Watt went on. "Everyone I've talked to is just wild about the idea," she said. "It was a positive inspiration. The white tuxedos, of course, will have to be made up specially. I've talked to a marvelous tailor. It will mean fittings. You and your father and your best man and Mr. Watt, Richie, can all go in together. That way, it will be taken care of in one fell swoop."

"I don't know about that," Richie said uncomfortably. "I'll feel like—"

"There is nothing sissy about white, Richie. Not at a wedding. Besides, with a white tux, you can always have it dyed later. If it were red or some other color, it might be a problem, but white takes the dye wonderfully." She addressed Emma again. "Remember that white party dress, when you were in the first grade?" she said. "We dyed that blue. It came out fine, didn't it? Tell Richie."

Emma sighed.

"She doesn't remember," Mrs. Watt told Richie. "But I do. And, believe me, you won't have any trouble at all dying your tux. I think we may be able to get the carnations from Hawaii. Wouldn't that be scrumptious?"

Richie blinked. The transition had been a bit too fast for him.

"The florist wouldn't promise," Mrs. Watt explained. "It has something to do with the rainfall in Oahu. I didn't quite understand. I never have had a green thumb. But, we'll hope for the best. Imported or domestic, he assures me that the angels will be divine."

"That's nice," Richie said apathetically.

"And a seven-layer cake, Richie, with just gobs of chiffon icing."

He brightened slightly. "Is that that sticky stuff?"

"Silky, I usually think of it as. Now, the guest list . . ."

Mrs. Watt rambled on for over an hour. She seemed completely unaware of Richie's and Emma's lack of interest in the details of the wedding. Richie did a great deal of nodding, even at times when no response was called for. Emma peered about the room, looking here and there, her mind seemingly in neutral. When she was asked for agreement, she agreed mechanically.

"You children have been dears," Mrs. Watt said, finally. "I don't know how I could have done this without you." She rose, beaming euphorically. "We'll all be *so* pleased, I'm sure. It will be the kind of wedding that every girl dreams of. And boy," she added, smiling at Richie. "You'll look so manly in white. Just like a knight."

"It's the knight's horse that's white, isn't it?" he said.

"No, dear, a white knight." She frowned thoughtfully. "But a white horse . . ." She shook her head. "No, I'm sure the American Legion would never allow that. And Emma's father! Never in a million years." She turned away. "Don't forget to tell your father about the fitting," she said to Richie, departing.

"Okay. . . ."

Richie and Emma sat in silence. Emma looked toward the windows again. Richie began cleaning one fingernail with another fingernail.

Then Emma spoke. "Richie, I'm sorry about what I said about you couldn't get into college."

"That's okay."

"I went to the telephone company a couple days ago to see about getting a job," she said. "They told me they'd let me know. The way they said it, though. . . . So, I started looking other places.

"It's not so casy."

Silence again.

"It's really going to be some wedding," Richie said.

"Uh-huh."

"I guess we better start looking for a ring," Richie said. "Do you want to go around some night and look?"

"We'll have to find out what size my mother wears," Emma said. "It's going to be her wedding."

Richie laughed. "Yeah."

"Maybe I'll talk to Millie and ask her how she got on at the telephone company," Emma said.

"Uhhhh . . . maybe you shouldn't just now," Richie said. "They're having some trouble."

"The telephone company? What?"

"No, Joe and Millie." He looked down at his fingers again. "Millie's going to have a baby. And Joe's— He's— He doesn't like kids or something."

"Oh, boy!"

"He was doing a lot of talking," Richie said. "But he'd had a couple beers. He'll be all right, I guess. I don't know. . . . He was blaming it on Millie. She quit her job, he said. He says she doesn't feel too well."

"Morning sickness, probably."

Richie nodded.

"If Millie quit her job, I guess they won't have her money any more."

"I guess not."

"Well . . . if Joe's working. . . ."

"Yeah, I guess they can get along. He probably won't talk about burning five dollar bills much more, though. It's getting a little late," he said. "I worked hard today." He rose. "Anyway. . . ."

Emma got up and followed him as he walked toward the entryway.

"I didn't mean anything about you and Bobby Scull," Richie said. "I was just getting worried about you— you'd been gone so long. And then you drove up."

"I probably shouldn't have," she said.

He didn't argue.

They went out the door, then stopped on the porch.

"Richie . . . you don't have to wear a white suit if you don't want to," Emma said. "I'll just tell my mother you're not going to. What can she do? She can't make you."

He shrugged. "I guess it's not important." He smiled faintly. "Well. . . ."

Emma leaned forward and kissed him lightly on the cheek.

"Goodnight," she said.

"I'll . . . uh. . . . We ought to do something about the ring, probably. Maybe tomorrow night . . . or the next night or sometime. . . ."

"There's plenty of time yet," Emma said.

"That's what I was thinking."

"Goodnight," she said again.

Richie nodded. "Goodnight."

On the way down the walk, Richie heard the screen door close. He stopped and looked back. Emma had gone in. He stood for a moment, as if he wanted to go back to the house and call Emma out again and tell her something. Then he shook his head, apparently having decided against it, and walked on. He walked slowly—very slowly.

NINE

Richie saw Mr. Starch chugging down the aisle toward him, where he was stacking cartons of Post Toasties. He guessed that the supervisor was on the trail of Joe Ferguson again. Oddly, though, he was wearing a slight smile, as if he were looking forward with pleasure to the prospect of finding Joe. Usually, his expression gave the impression that although he was searching diligently for Ferguson, his hope was that he would never ever again set eyes on him.

"Seen him?" the supervisor asked sharply, as he neared Richie.

"You mean—"

"If you see him, tell him I want him in my office," Mr. Starch said, going by.

"Are you talking about—"

But the supervisor had reached the end of the aisle and was gone.

Richie resumed stacking the featherweight cartons.

A moment later, Joe Ferguson appeared in the aisle, coming from the same direction that the supervisor had. Joe was ambling along, Whistling softly. As he approached Richie, he stopped whistling and broke out in the watermelon grin. He looked like the Joe

Ferguson whom Richie had met on his first day on the job.

"I think Mr. Starch is looking for you," Richie said.

"Sure he is," Joe replied. "He overshot me over in tomatoes. This is the way to steer clear of him—stay one step behind him."

"You and Millie must be all right again," Richie said, pleased, taking note of Joe Ferguson's cheerful manner.

"Couldn't be better," Joe told him. "We split up."

"You're joking, aren't you?" Richie said.

"No. She went home to her mother last night. It's finished. Kaput. It was fun while it lasted, Rich, but nothing goes on forever. She was too dumb for me. I'll tell you one thing, I'll never make that mistake again. I like a dame that's hot stuff, but she's got to have some brains, too. See what I mean?"

"What're you going to do now?" Richie asked, subdued.

"Start getting around again," Joe told him. "I saw some real cuties when Millie and we were making the rounds. But I couldn't do anything about it. I'm that kind of guy—one dame at a time."

"I meant, what are you and Millie going to do?"

"Divorce. What else?"

"I guess so. . . ." Richie said.

"It's not *all* Millie's fault," Joe said. "I should've seen through her. She really had me going, Richie. I thought she was my kind of dame. But, she turned out to be just like all the others."

"How?"

"What do you mean, how? Don't you see it? As soon as she thought she had her hooks in me, she started having babies. They all do that. Before, they'll tell you anything. They'll do anything you want. But once they get that marriage license, all bets are off. Look at what Millie did to me. There's the proof, isn't it?" He looked at Richie closely. "Didn't you say something to me the other day about you getting married?"

Richie nodded. "I didn't think you were listening."

"That what's-her-name?"

"Emma."

"Watch yourself, Richie. She'll do it to you," Joe told him. "That's their game. Want me to tell you something? They think they can hold onto you that way. Sure. It's been going on forever. You know, you get married, then you get the wandering eye after a while, and they see it, and they get scared. So, they start having kids. They think that'll hold you."

"I guess it could happen that way," Richie said. "But—"

"No buts. Look at my case. I started looking the cuties over and right away Millie gets pregnant. You think that was a coincidence? Don't kid yourself, Richie. But, the way I see it, an eye for an eye."

"What do you mean?"

"Well, she did me dirty, so, tit for tat. Get what I mean? Don't be a sucker. They think all they have to do is have kids and they've got you hog-tied for life. That's their game. But you can beat it. Don't be a sucker."

"What're you going to do about the baby, though?" Richie asked. "It's yours."

"Slips don't count, Richie. If I'd wanted a kid, it would be different. But I didn't want a kid. She made her bed, let her lay in it."

"But won't they make you—"

Mr. Starch had appeared again at the far end of the aisle.

"Oh-oh," Richie said. "There he is—right behind you."

"What can he do?" Joe said, unconcerned. "He's small potatoes, Richie. I've got Charles M. Coogan behind me."

The supervisor was approaching.

"But if you and Millie aren't going to be married any more," Richie said, "that might change things."

"How? It's not my fault. Fair's fair, Richie. He can't blame me for that. I didn't get pregnant."

Mr. Starch arrived. "Ferguson!"

Joe turned, grinning. "Hi, Mr. Starch. Glad you came along. I was just telling Cunningham here how we got to get the lead out. He's going to be on this truck of Post Toasties all morning if he doesn't get a move on. I'd be glad if you'd back me up. You know how these kids are."

"Get a move on, there," the supervisor said to Richie.

"Yes, sir."

"Ferguson, you come with me," Mr. Starch said. "I want to see you in my office."

"I'm seeing Charles M. Coogan this morning," Joe told him.

"Oh, you are, are you? Charles M. Coogan isn't here. So maybe you can spare a second for me."

"As a matter of fact, I've been wanting to get together with you," Joe said. "I was talking to Charles M. Coogan the other day—"

"Let's go, Ferguson."

They walked toward the end of the aisle.

"—and I was telling him how we can get a little more ginger out of these kids," Joe went on. "They're good kids, but they don't know anything about responsibility. They'd bleed us white if we let them. I told Charles M. Coogan that what he ought to do is boost you up the ladder, and that would leave the way open for somebody . . .'

They moved beyond Richie's range of hearing, then reached the end of the aisle and passed from sight.

Richie began stacking the cartons of Post Toasties again. Now, strangely, they felt heavy.

When Richie got off the bus that afternoon, returning from work, he started toward home, but then detoured and walked in the direction of the park. His hope was that he would find a baseball game going on. He intended to join it. He needed to do something to get his mind off Joe and Millie Ferguson and his own fast-approaching marriage.

There was no game. But Potsie and Ralph were in the park. They were lying on the grass in the shade of a tree, with their bikes lying nearby.

"What's new? Richie asked, sitting down on the grass beside them.

"School," Potsie said glumly.

"What about it?"

"Vacation's almost over," Ralph said.

"It's still a few weeks."

'The last weeks go like sixty," Potsie said. "We ought to be doing something. The vacation's going to be gone, and what've we done?"

"Why don't you do something?" Richie said.

"What?"

"I don't know. What about all that stuff you said you were going to do when vacation started? Have you done it?"

Potsie was silent for a moment. Then he said, "I don't remember what it was." He looked toward Ralph. "Do you remember?"

"We were going on that camping trip."

"We ought to do that," Potsie said.

"Ahhhh . . . I don't feel like it."

"Who's going with who?" Richie asked.

"I don't know," Potsie replied. "You know, Ralph?"

Ralph shook his head. "I haven't been out to the beach."

"We got to do something," Potsie said. "You know what comes next, don't you? Getting up every morning. Going to school."

"Memorizing dates," Ralph said painfully.

"How do you know you'll get Mrs. McCormack?" Richie asked.

"My luck."

"That's a crime," Potsie said. "Making high school guys memorize dates. What does she think we are, kids? We did that in grade school."

"Same dates, too," Ralph said. "It shouldn't be hard, you'd think. But I forgot them from when I was in grade school."

"You're lucky, Richie," Potsie said. "You don't have to worry about starting to get up to go to school every day."

"I have to get up to go to work. I've been doing it all summer."

"Yeah, but you're used to it."

"You don't have to memorize dates," Ralph said to Richie.

"You don't have to lug around a lot of canned peas," Richie countered.

"You'll be married," Potsie said.

Richie did not respond.

"Boy, you know, when you think about that . . ." Potsie said. "No more school. Never again. No more math. No more Latin." He turned toward Richie. "There you are. Which would you rather do, conjugate a Latin verb or carry peas?"

Richie shrugged. "Latin's not so bad."

"Since when?"

"Since . . . I don't know. . . ."

"I'll carry peas any day," Ralph said.

"How about geometry?" Potsie said.

"Yeah, how about geometry?" Ralph said.

"Geometry's not so bad."

"Because you're finished with it," Potsie said. "You don't ever have to ever go to another geometry class. I wouldn't think it was so bad, either, if I didn't ever have to do it again."

"Give me peas," Ralph said.

"How many cases of canned peas have you ever lifted?" Richie asked.

"I carried a case of canned beets in once from the car," Ralph said. "My mother got it on sale."

"Try doing it all day," Richie said.

Silence.

"It'd build up your muscles," Potsie said. "You can't say that for geometry."

"Or Latin," Ralph said.

"I'll trade you my muscles—" Richie began. He

sighed and looked off toward the distance. "I guess I better get going," he said.

"Something on?" Potsie asked.

"No, nothing special. Just eat supper and then go over to Emma's. We might go look for a ring tonight." He rose. "I'll see you guys."

"See you," Potsie said.

"Don't drop any peas," Ralph said.

"Yeah."

Walking toward home, Richie felt as if he were carrying on his shoulders all the cartons he had lifted all summer. When he reached the edge of the park, he halted. He stood for several minutes. Various thoughts drifted through his mind, none of them ever becoming whole. Then he moved on—but going in a different direction, away from home.

The house was dark except for the lights in the living room when Richie finally reached there that night. He hesitated before entering, knowing that he would find his parents waiting for him. He practiced making nonchalant faces and he gestured casually several times, just to make sure that he could do it with ease. Then he went in.

His mother came running to meet him and his father was not far behind.

"Richie, where have you been!" his mother demanded, partly angry, partly worried. "Do you know what time it is!"

"Not exactly."

"Where have you been, Richie?" his father asked calmly.

"For a walk."

"A walk!" his mother said. "All this time? Where to? Why?

"I walked out to the filtration plant," Richie told her. "It takes a while."

"What's going on out there?" Howard Cunningham asked.

"Nothing. I just felt like thinking. And I just went out there and sat on the hill."

His mother's manner softened. "We were worried," she said. "Emma was worried, too. I called her—I thought you might be there. But you weren't, of course. And, since then, she's called here twice. Richie . . . are you all right?"

"Sure."

"What were you thinking about?"

"Marion. . . ." Howard Cunningham said.

She looked at her husband, then faced Richie again. "Well, all right," she said, "as long as you're safe. I suppose I can go to bed now. But I think you ought to telephone Emma. She's as worried as I was."

"I will."

His mother walked toward the stairs. "Goodnight, dear."

" 'Night, Mom."

When she had gone, Richie's father went back into the living room and Richie went to the phone and called Emma:

Richie: Hi, it's me.

Emma: Where were you?"

Richie: I went for a walk.

(silence)

Richie: I had a long day, that's all. Joe and Millie are getting a divorce.

Emma: Oh. That's too bad. I guess it is, anyway. I don't know.

Richie: I'll see you tomorrow night.

Emma: Are you all right, Richie?

Richie: I'm tired, that's about all.

Emma: See you tomorrow, then. Goodnight.

Richie: 'Night.

He hung up and walked into the living room and dropped into a chair and slid down.

"How're things at the waterworks?" his father asked amiably.

"Okay."

"Wheel still going around?"

Richie nodded.

"I worry about that," Howard Cunningham said. "Remember when it stopped and we couldn't get water? I had to shave with Coca-Cola. There's nothing like shaving with soda pop to make a man appreciate the marvels of the mechanical age."

Richie smiled weakly. "Dad, when you and mom were going to get married," he said, "were you sure you wanted to?"

"That's a long way back, Richie. I don't remember all of the details. I probably had some doubts as the last minute approached. Your mother probably did, too. Are you going through that?"

"Yeah."

"Do you want to have one of those father-and-son talks?"

"I don't know."

"If they're getting to be too much for you, I could be the son this time and you could be the father."

"No . . ." Richie pushed himself up in the chair. "The thing is, I want to get married and I don't."

"Uh-huh. Richie, there's a thing called the sex urge. I'm sure you know what it is. Maybe, though, you don't know how powerful it can be sometimes . . . especially when you're young. It can make you think you want things that maybe, if it weren't for that urge, you might not want at all."

"You mean that's why I asked Emma to marry me?"

"I can't answer that, Richie," his father replied. "Only you know whether it was that . . . or if you're really in love with her and honestly are ready to take on marriage."

"I *don't* know, though," Richie said. "That's what I was thinking about, sort of. But I didn't get any answer. See, I don't know if I'm in love with Emma or not. One minute, I think I am, and the next minute, I'm not. There's this guy at work. Whenever he does something, he switches it around and tries to make it look like somebody else is to blame. And, thinking, I found out I was trying to do that, too. Put the blame for everything on Emma, I mean. So, I don't know what's what."

"Right now, I'm not even sure I know what the question is, let alone the answer," his father said.

"Am I in love with Emma? I don't know."

"Do you like her?"

"Sure, I like her well enough. What's that got to do with it?"

"Quite a bit, I think. Loving begins with liking, Richie. Sex, though, that can begin with anything.

The way a girl moves her head . . . or the way she looks at you . . . or even a lot less than that. But there's a little more to liking. I wish I could explain liking to you. But it has a lot to do with feeling . . . and I don't know all the right words for it. I know it's more, though, than how a girl holds her head or the way she looks at you. You can get tired of that if that's all there is. But I don't think you can ever really get tired of someone you really like."

"Well, as I say, I like Emma. I'm not tired of her or anything."

"Do you like her well enough to spend the rest of your life with her?"

"Twenty-four hours a day?"

"You know what I mean, Richie."

"I'm not sure."

"I don't expect you to be sure. I'm asking you what you think."

"I like being with her now," Richie said.

"What do you do when you're together?"

"You know."

"Neck?"

"Well, sure, sometimes."

"What do you think about what your mother and I do when we're together. When you see us together, that is," Howard asked. "Pretty dull stuff?"

"Well, you're older."

"You're going to get older, Richie. So is Emma. This may sound preposterous to you now, but, believe it or not, someday you and Emma are going to be as old as your mother and I are now."

"In about a million years, maybe, but—"

"I hate to be a killjoy, but it'll happen a lot faster

than that. And, long before that, Richie, you'll discover that you can't possibly fill your entire day with sex. You'll have quite a few hours where you'll have to think of something else to do. If you *like* each other, that's no problem at all. If you *don't* like each other—if sex is the only thing you've got—you're in a bad, bad fix."

Richie frowned thoughtfully. "Gee, I wonder what else we could do?"

"You won't have to think of things. Remember the other night when your mother and I were up late trying to squeeze a vacation trip out of the budget? Things like that are coming up all the time. I know, you thought it was a little senile, putting a couple bucks over here, another couple bucks over there. But—and you'll probably find this hard to believe, too—we enjoy it. Why? I don't know. Maybe just because we're doing it together and we like doing things together."

Richie looked perplexed.

"These father-and-son talks are overrated," Howard said. "I'm not helping you at all."

"No, that's okay," Richie said. "Only I still don't know if I'm in love with Emma or not. I don't even know how much I like her now." He suddenly looked panicky.

"Richie, what's the matter?"

"I just thought of something. You don't suppose she'll turn out to be like her mother, do you?"

"I have no way of knowing. But Mrs. Watt is nice."

"I wouldn't want to be married to somebody who made me stand around in a corner being a lamp all the time. I remember . . . when we were talking about an apartment once, Emma already knew where she wanted the pictures—right behind the pull-out couch—and the kind she wanted, too. Give her a week, I bet, and she'd be moving those pictures around."

"That's something you could live with, I'm sure."

"I don't know. I like the furniture to stay where it is," Richie said. "Like ours. We don't move our furniture around. It's been the same place as long as I can remember."

"You're aging faster than I expected you to, Richie," his father said. "You may be older than I am already."

"No, that's something to think about," Richie said. "Suppose I came home some night and Emma'd moved a chair or something and I fell over it and broke a leg?"

"Richie, are you secretly a writer for Milton Berle? That happens an awful lot on his show."

"It *could* happen," Richie insisted.

"I won't say that it couldn't."

"And what if we had children?" Richie went on.

"With your leg in a cast?"

"I mean what if we had children and Emma turned out to be like her mother, moving the furniture around all the time? That'd be an awful mess. We'd be fighting about the furniture. And we couldn't do anything about it because we'd have the kids."

"You've changed your mind about getting married, I take it."

"I don't know. I'm just thinking about things that could happen. Marriage is serious."

"Yes, but I don't think a little thing like moving furniture—"

"Little things lead to big things."

"What do you have in mind? World War III?"

"Dad, I just want to be mature about it."

"It sounds to me like you're looking for an excuse—and you'll take the first one that comes along."

"No, that's not it," Richie said, rising. "I just want to be fair. Emma wouldn't be happy either."

"That's true . . . you with your broken leg, fighting about the furniture, the children, World War III . . . I don't see much to be optimistic about."

"I'll still think it over a while," Richie said, backing out of the room. "But, the way it looks. . . ."

"It's too bad," Howard Cunningham said. "I was looking forward to seeing myself in a white tuxedo."

"Nothing's settled."

"Goodnight, Richie."

" 'Night."

Richie trotted up the stairs. But by the time he reached his room, his revived spirits were beginning to wane again. He was thinking about Joe Ferguson. How Joe had managed to put the blame on Millie for the breakup of their marriage. Wasn't he, Richie, doing the same thing? Breaking up with Emma because at some time in the future she might just possibly start moving the furniture around? No wonder his father hadn't believed him when he had called it fair. He was like Joe, thinking about nobody but himself.

He was trapped, he decided. He couldn't break up with Emma. Because Emma was in love with him. And he had asked her to marry him. He couldn't back out, he couldn't hurt her like that. The only thing he could do was go through with it—white monkey suit and all.

TEN

Richie was stacking cartons of canned yams when he saw Phil Mackey coming toward him along the aisle. Mackey was one of the young men who worked on the loading dock. He was broad-shouldered and ruddy-faced. In general appearance, however, he looked somewhat different this morning. He was wearing a tie and carrying a clipboard. And, overnight, he had acquired the facial expression of authority. Mackey looked dead serious.

"Cunningham?" Mackey said, arriving.

Richie nodded, perplexed. The young man had always called him by his first name before.

"What're you doing here?" Mackey asked, looking at the truckload of yam cartons.

"Uhhh . . . stacking yams," Richie replied.

Mackey consulted the clipboard. "All right . . . I'm putting you down here for yams," he said, making a note with a stub of a pencil. "We've got a couple big loads coming in today, so keep on your toes."

"I'm almost finished with the yams," Richie pointed out. "After that, there's a load of prune juice."

"When'll you be over in prune juice?"

"I don't know . . . when I finish with the yams."

"You better let me know when you go over to prune juice," Mackey said. "I'm keeping track. I want to know where everybody is at every minute. That's the only way to get things done."

"You want me to look for you?" Richie asked.

Mackey nodded. "Look me up."

"What if I can't find you? Should I just go on over to the prunes"

"No, check in first. I've got you down for yams right now. If you go on over to prune juice, and don't check in, I won't know where you are."

"I'll be in prune juice."

"But I won't know that, Richie. On my chart here, see, it'll say yams."

"Why don't you write down 'yams *or* prune juice'?" Richie suggested.

"I've already got 'yams' down here. You better just check in with me before you go on over to prune juice."

"Phil, what're you doing?" Richie asked.

"Keeping a chart."

"How come, I mean?" Richie asked.

"So I'll know where all you guys are. If I need you, all I'll have to do is look at my chart and I can go right to where you are."

"How come you're doing it, though?"

"I guess you didn't hear," Mackey replied. "I'm taking over Joe's job."

Richie's eyes opened wide in surprise. "Did Joe get a boost up?"

Mackey chuckled. "He got a boost, all right," he replied. "He got a boost right out the door. Starch fired him yesterday."

"How could he—" The answer suddenly became

obvious. Having decided to divorce Millie, Joe Ferguson no longer had Charles M. Coogan's protection. "Just fired him, huh?" he said. "Just like that. . . ."

"He wasn't doing the job, Richie. You know that."

"Yeah. . . ."

"He had this chart all along and he never used it," Mackey said.

Richie nodded.

"Keep on your toes," Mackey said, going on. "And don't forget, let me know before you go over to prune juice."

"Sure."

When Mackey had gone, Richie sat down on a carton of yams. He felt unhappy for Joe Ferguson, even though, clearly, Joe had deserved to lose the job. Then he began to feel unhappy for himself. The supervisor had practically told him that he would get Joe's job if Joe were let go. Why Mackey? Why not Richie?

Richie got up and left the yams and went to the supervisor's office. Mr. Starch was at his desk, invoices spread out before him. Richie stood in the doorway. The supervisor was unaware of him. So Richie cleared his throat. The supervisor raised his eyes from the invoices and looked at Richie vaguely, as if trying to place him.

"Could I talk to you a minute?" Richie asked.

"What is it, Moorhouse?"

"I'm Cunningham, sir. Richie Cunningham."

"Right. Come in. What's on your mind?"

"I was just talking to Phil Mackey and he told me you fired Joe Ferguson and gave him his job."

Starch smiled blissfully. "Yes, I finally got rid of that

loafer. Charles M. Coogan wised up to him. I knew it would happen." The smile faded. "What about it?"

"Well, a couple weeks ago . . . a few weeks ago . . . we were talking, you and me, and you told me how I've got a great future here and— You sort of promised me Joe's job."

The supervisor looked blank. "I don't remember that."

"You didn't say it in so many words," Richie admitted. "But I was kind of counting on it. I decided not to go back to school, on account of have this great future here. So, I was wondering."

"You've still got a great future, Moorhouse. Just—"

"Cunningham, sir."

"Cunningham, right. You've still got a great future. Keep your nose to the grindstone and your shoulder to the wheel and you can go right to the top around here. I keep my eyes on you boys. You're like my own kids. I've got a lot of pride in you. Take my word for it, when it's time for you to move up, you'll move up."

"I could handle Joe's job right now," Richie said.

"Maybe you could," Starch replied. "But there's more to it than that. That's a man's job. You're still a kid. We've got a rule around here, Cunningham: never send a kid to do a man's job. Think about it. It makes sense."

"But what about my great future?" Richie asked.

"I think we've got a misunderstanding here," Starch said. "You're thinking 'great' and I'm thinking 'future.' Future, you know, that doesn't mean today. That means tomorrow, or next week or next month or next year or sometime. Or, it could mean never. It all depends on you, Cunningham. Do your job, don't make waves, stay in line, and you'll get what's coming to you—when the time comes."

"Yes, sir."

"Satisfied?"

"Well, there isn't any misunderstanding anymore," Richie replied.

"Good. Now, get out there and get that nose to that grindstone, boy. That's the way to do it. You've got a great future here."

Richie returned to work. He found that he was not disappointed. In fact, it was somewhat of a relief to discover that he didn't really have a great future at Mid-State. If he decided to quit the job at the end of summer and return to school—not that he had any thought of doing that, but just in case—he wouldn't be leaving anything of any value or promise behind.

Emma was alone when Richie arrived at the Watt house that evening.

"They went to a movie," she said, leading the way into the living room.

"What're they seeing?"

Emma thought for a moment. "I don't remember. They told me, but . . . I've had a lot on my mind."

Richie sat down on the sofa. "Me, too. Joe got fired yesterday," he said. "I found out today when I went in to work."

Emma settled in a chair. "He's getting everything at once, isn't he?" she said.

"Yeah." He looked around the room, avoiding Emma's eyes. "We're supposed to go look for a ring, I guess, aren't we?" he said.

"Richie, I was thinking about that. It's been so hot

lately. My fingers swell up in hot weather. Maybe we ought to wait a while. If we bought a ring now, in hot weather, it might not fit later on."

"That's something to think about," Richie agreed. "Maybe the weather will let up soon."

"Sure. It'd be crazy to get a ring now and then have it not fit and have to take it back and have it . . . whatever they do. . . ."

"Adjust it."

He nodded. "Listen, I told you about Joe getting fired, you know? Well, they gave one of the other guys his job. I thought I'd probably get it. Did I mention that?"

"Weren't you kind of counting on it?"

"Sort of. I had a talk with the supervisor today. You know, Emma, I'm not so sure anymore that I've got such a great future there."

"Did he say that?"

"He didn't exactly *say* it. But I got the feeling."

"What did he say exactly?"

"That I've still got a great future there. But it was the way he said it."

Emma nodded. "I know what you mean. I've been hearing a lot of things like that, looking for a job. People say one thing, but they mean something else. Why do they do that?"

"Search me."

"A lot of them tell me I'm too young," Emma said. "I don't know what they *really* mean. I'm not too young."

"Yeah, that supervisor said something to me today about being a kid," Richie told her. "He sat there and said it with a straight face. They just think up excuses."

"You know what I was thinking?" Emma said.

"What?"

"Well, maybe I shouldn't tell you."

"No, go ahead."

"You won't get the wrong idea, will you?"

"No."

"Well, I was thinking. . . . I'm just not having any luck at all getting a job. So, I was thinking. . . . School will be starting soon. If I don't get a job by then, I was thinking, maybe I ought to go back. Not to stay," she said hastily. "Just to give me something to do until I get a job. I'll keep looking. Of course, I'll probably find a job *before* school starts. But, in case I don't, you know."

"That wouldn't hurt," Richie said. "It would give you something to do, instead of just hanging around."

"That's what I was thinking. And, like I say, I can still look for a job . . . when I get a chance. . . ."

"You know what I've been thinking?" Richie said.

"What?" she asked expectantly.

"Don't take this wrong."

"No, I won't, I promise."

"Well, since we can't get the ring yet. And it doesn't look like I'll be getting a raise at work very soon. And you haven't found a job yet. We'd be awful short on money. And—"

"And an apartment and furniture's going to cost a lot," Emma said. "Even if we bought the furniture on time."

"Do you know it actually costs *more* when you buy it on time?" Richie told her.

"It does?"

"They charge you."

"That's not very nice," Emma said, mildly indignant. "But what were you saying?"

"What I was going to say was—taking everything into account, you know—maybe we ought to put off getting married for a while."

"That might be smart," Emma replied.

"Just for a little while."

"Oh, sure."

"I might even look around for a better job or something," Richie said. "Better paying. All the really high-paying jobs go to high school graduates, though."

"Richie, I've got an idea," Emma said. "You could go back to school, too, when it opens. It'd be best for both of us in the long run. If you got your high school diploma, you could get a high-paying job, then we wouldn't have to buy the furniture on time."

"I'd be a big saving," Richie said. "We wouldn't have to pay the charges." He paused. "But, then, we wouldn't be getting married for a long time."

"I guess there's no rush," Emma said. "Unless you're in a big hurry."

"No, what the heck. We'll still be engaged . . . or, as good as, anyway."

"We could just call it going steady," Emma suggested.

"Sure."

"But, you know what a lot of kids are doing these days?" Emma said. "They're going steady, but they're still dating, too."

"How can they do that?" Richie asked, puzzled.

"You can do anything you want to. It's a free country, isn't it?

"I guess . . . but, I don't see how—"

"The idea is, it's a lot better to go out with a lot of

people instead of just one," Emma explained. "It's better preparation."

"For what?"

"For marriage. Don't you see? If you only go out with one person, that's all you know. But if you go out with a lot of people, you get to know a lot of different kinds. Then, when you're ready to get married, you've had that experience. You're more ready to settle down."

"That's probably what was the matter with Joe—he wasn't ready to settle down," Richie said.

"I'll bet you're right."

"I wouldn't want that to happen to us."

"Me, neither."

"Okay, we'll go steady that way," Richie said.

Emma laughed. "It's sounds kind of dumb, though, saying you're going steady, when you're going out with other people. And, too, you know if you say you're going steady, and you're a girl, a lot of boys won't ask you out. That would ruin it."

"Ruin what?"

"The whole idea, Richie, is to get the experience. Otherwise, why bother? How can I get the experience, though, if everybody thinks I'm going steady and nobody asks me out?"

"I guess we'll just have to go steady and not tell anybody," Richie said.

"And go out with other people."

"It would probably work out better that way," Richie agreed.

"It still sounds silly, though, doesn't it?" Emma said.

"I wouldn't want any of the guys to find out," Richie said. "Boy, they'd kid the pants off me."

"Richie, maybe we ought to be just good friends."

"Hey! Yeah!"

From outside, came the sound of the Watt car pulling into the driveway.

"That's them," Emma said.

Richie groaned. "Now, we've got to tell your mother. Boy, I don't know . . . she really has her heart set on those white suits."

"I'll tell her," Emma said.

Richie rose. "Maybe I'll go, then."

Emma got up. "Richie . . . ," she said softly, ". . . it was still a nice summer . . ."

"It was great," he said. "Except for my job."

She kissed him affectionately. "Goodnight. . . ."

There was the sound of the screen door opening. Then the Watts appeared in the entryway. Mrs. Watt was crying.

"Emma, you should have seen it," she said. "It was beautiful. So tragic." She ran for the stairs.

"What happened?" Emma asked her father.

"William Holden shot himself in the swimming pool," he told her.

When Richie entered the house, whistling, his father was sitting in the living room reading the evening paper.

Richie paused in the doorway. "The wedding's off," he told Howard Cunningham.

"I can't say that I'm greatly surprised. Did you finally come up with a right reason?"

"Oh, sure. Emma's fingers swell up in hot weather."

Richie moved on to the stairs, whistling again.

His father looked off into space, pondering. Then

he spoke aloud. "He *does* have a lot of his Uncle Frank in him," he said.

"Who says you have to save it all for college?" Potsie said to Richie, as, a few nights later, they sat in a booth inside the drive-in.

"Nobody says," Richie replied. "That's what I worked all summer for—to save up for college."

"But wait'll you see this jalopy this guy's got," Potsie said. "It's a steal."

"I don't want a jalopy."

"Everybody wants a jalopy," Potsie said.

"Okay, maybe I want one. But I've got to save that money. I told everybody I was."

"You told everybody you were getting married, too," Potsie argued. "If you can chicken out on that—"

"I didn't chicken out."

"Okay, do you want to look at this guy's jalopy?"

Richie looked past him. Ralph was approaching the booth and he was grinning smugly.

"Guess who's outside in Bobby Scull's car," Ralph said, joining Richie and Potsie in the booth.

"Who?" Potsie asked.

"That's not Bobby Scull's car, it's his dad's," Richie said.

"He's driving it."

"That doesn't make it his car. Guys drive buses, too, but that doesn't make them their buses," Richie said.

"Who?" Potsie asked again.

"Richie knows," Ralph said. "Ask him."

"Who?" Potsie asked Richie.

"How do I know? I'm sitting here with you."

"Who?" Potsie asked Ralph.

"He knows," Ralph said.

"How would I know?"

"Emma," Ralph told Potsie.

"Oh." He was disappointed. "Just take a look at this jalopy," he said to Richie.

"No dice."

"Bobby Scull'll be going back to college," Potsie said. "When he goes, you could be one of the few guys with transportation. Maybe you could get Emma back."

"We called it quits."

"Sure. But if you had this jalopy, she might change her mind."

"It didn't have anything to do with that," Richie said.

"How do you know?" Potsie asked. "There's only one way to find out—get the jalopy."

"Why'd she drop you, then?" Ralph asked Richie.

"She didn't."

"Are you saying you dropped her? Emma?"

"We just decided to call it off," Richie told him.

Mitch joined them. "Guess who's out in front in Bobby Scull's car," he said.

Silence.

Mitch looked around at the faces. He shrugged and picked up the menu card.

"You'll be seeing her with Richie again before long," Potsie said to Mitch. "He's getting a jalopy."

"I'm not either," Richie said.

Tom, in his capacity as a waiter, stopped at the booth. "What do you guys want?" he asked.

"We're thinking," Ralph told him.

"You guys've got to order something," Tom told them.

"We're thinking."

"Okay, but don't think all night."

"That's what happens when a guy puts on a uniform," Mitch said, as Tom departed.

Potsie leaned out of the booth, looking after Tom. "All he's got on is that white apron," he said.

"That's a uniform."

"How can it be a uniform? It ties in the back."

Mitch ignored the question. He focused his attention on Richie. "You going out and start something with Bobby Scull?" he said.

"What for? It's a free country."

"If he stole my girl. . . ." He did not complete the thought.

"He didn't steal anybody," Potsie told Mitch. "Richie dropped her."

"No, I didn't," Richie said. "We decided together."

"Come on. . . ." Mitch said.

"No kidding."

Mitch fixed his eyes on the menu card again. "Maybe, after Bobby Scull goes back to college, I'll take her out," he said. "Think I should?"

Richie shrugged. "That's up to you."

"Is it worth it, I mean?" Mitch said, his eyes still on the menu.

"How?"

"You know. You were as good as engaged, weren't you? You must know."

"Listen, if you're thinking something, you're wrong," Richie told him. "Nothing went on."

"Sure," Mitch said.

"Listen, Mitch—"

Potsie broke in. "I could get this guy to drive that jalopy around to your house," he said to Richie. "He'd be glad to. You wouldn't have to buy. You could just look."

"What good would that do? That money's put away."

"You were as good as engaged all summer almost," Mitch said to Richie. "You must have done something."

"Sure we did. But not what you think."

"What'd you do?"

"Just stuff."

"Here comes Tom," Ralph said.

"I'll get a Coke," Mitch said, putting the menu down. "You guys split the cost?"

The others nodded.

"Come on, Richie, what'd you do?" Mitch said. "Don't tell me it was the same as just hanging around. What was it like?"

"No, it wasn't the same."

"He stopped at that other booth," Ralph said, reporting on Tom.

"What *was* it like, then?" Mitch persisted.

Richie frowned meditatively.

Mitch, Ralph and Potsie leaned forward, waiting.

"Come on," Mitch said again.

"Well . . . ," Richie said.

"Don't you know? The whole summer and you don't even know?"

"Sure, I know."

"Then, how was it?"

"Unforgettable," Richie told them.

As one, they sagged.

Tom arrived at the booth. "What are you guys going to have?" he asked.

"A Coke," Mitch told him.

Tom looked at Potsie.

"I'm just sitting here with Mitch," Potsie told him.

"Me, too," Richie said.

"Same here," Ralph said.

"Cut it out, you guys," Tom said. "You can't just order one Coke and take up a whole booth. The boss'll jump all over me."

"You ought to get some brass buttons for that apron," Potsie said.

"What's that mean?"

"That's for me to know and you to find out."

"Come on, are you going to order?" Tom said.

"Okay, two Cokes," Richie said. "Ralph's sitting with Mitch and Potsie's sitting with me."

"Cheap," Tom said, leaving with the order.

They all looked after him.

"They must have made him a partner," Mitch said.

"Hey, Richie, you know what?" Potsie said. "Maybe you could get that guy to sell you that jalopy on time. That way, you could keep your savings."

"Tell you what," Richie said. "A guy I used to work with owes me ten bucks. He told me he put a check in the mail. When it comes, we'll go look at that jalopy."

"Now, you're talking," Potsie said. "You won't be sorry, either. This is a great-looking jalopy. Wait'll Emma sees it."

"Will you forget about Emma? That's over."

"You never know," Ralph said. "Bobby Scull'll be going back to college soon."

"Okay," Richie said, defeated, "you guys want to know the truth? She dropped me."

Why didn't you say so?" Potsie said.

"Now, you know—okay?"

There were nods.

"You guys want to chip in and put something in the juke box?" Mitch asked.

They began digging for nickels.

GENERAL FICTION

0352	Star	
	Michael J. Bird	
301481	**WHO PAYS THE FERRYMAN?**	85p ♦
	William Burroughs	
39613X	**DEAD FINGERS TALK**	75p
	Jackie Collins	
395621	**THE STUD**	65p
300701	**LOVEHEAD**	70p
398663	**THE WORLD IS FULL OF DIVORCED WOMEN**	50p
398752	**THE WORLD IS FULL OF MARRIED MEN**	50p
	Robertson Davies	
396113	**FIFTH BUSINESS**	95p
	Alexander Edwards	
396881	**A STAR IS BORN**	60p ♦
	Robert Grossbach	
30166X	**THE GOODBYE GIRL**	60p* ♦
	W. Harris	
301406	**SALIVA**	70p
	Dan Jenkins	
302100	**SEMI-TOUGH**	75p* ♦
	Jeffrey Konvitz	
398981	**THE SENTINEL**	70p* ♦
	Dean R. Koontz	
301643	**NIGHT CHILLS**	75p*
	Lee Mackenzie	
396903	**EMMERDALE FARM (No. 1) THE LEGACY**	50p ♦
396296	**EMMERDALE FARM (No. 2) PRODIGAL'S PROGRESS**	60p ♦
395974	**EMMERDALE FARM (No. 3) ALL THAT A MAN HAS . . .**	60p ♦
301414	**EMMERDALE FARM (No. 4) LOVERS' MEETING**	60p ♦
301422	**EMMERDALE FARM (No. 5) A SAD AND HAPPY SUMMER**	60p ♦
	Graham Masterton	
396164	**THE MANITOU**	70p ♦
395265	**THE DJINN**	75p*

† For sale in Britain and Ireland only.
*Not for sale in Canada.
♦ Film & T.V. tie-ins.

GENERAL FICTION

		Robert Stone	
0352	397403	DOG SOLDIERS	75p*
		Peter Upton	
	395427	GREEN HILL FAR AWAY	95p
		Margaret Walker	
	30157 0	JUBILEE	95p*
		N. Richard Nash	
	301562	EAST WIND, RAIN	95p*
		Gail Parent	
	395540	DAVID MEYER IS A MOTHER	70p
		Molly Parkin	
	300809	LOVE ALL	50p
	397179	UP TIGHT	60p
		Erich Maria Remarque	
	396288	BOBBY DEERFIELD	85p* ♦
		Judith Rossner	
	396946	TO THE PRECIPICE	85p*
	302089	NINE MONTHS IN THE LIFE OF AN OLD MAID	75p*
		Alan Sillitoe	
	398892	THE GENERAL	50p
	300965	THE LONELINESS OF THE LONG-DISTANCE RUNNER	50p
	300949	MEN, WOMEN AND CHILDREN	50p
	300981	SATURDAY NIGHT AND SUNDAY MORNING	50p
	395141	THE WIDOWER'S SON	85p
	397144	THE FLAME OF LIFE	70p
	398809	THE RAGMAN'S DAUGHTER	50p
		Hubert Selby Jr.	
	396415	THE ROOM	75p

† For sale in Britain and Ireland only.
*Not for sale in Canada.
♦ Film & T.V. tie-ins.

GENERAL FICTION

0426 Universal / Tandem

	Catherine Cookson	
163796	**THE GARMENT**	70p
163524	**HANNAH MASSEY**	70p
163605	**SLINKY JANE**	70p
	Brian Hayles	
165209	**SPRING AT BROOKFIELD**	70p
	William Johnston	
183746	**HAPPY DAYS: THE FONZ AND LAZONGA**	70p* ♦
183827	**THE BIKE TYCOON**	70p* ♦
18438 6	**DEAR FONZIE . . .**	70p* ♦
185346	**FONZIE GOES TO COLLEGE**	70p* ♦
	John Kershaw	
18577 3	**ROOMS**	75p ♦
	Keith Miles	
16539X	**AMBRIDGE SUMMER**	70p
	Fiona Richmond	
181980	**THE STORY OF I**	75p
	Betty Smith	
178815	**JOY IN THE MORNING**	70p*
179455	**MAGGIE: NOW**	75p*
178734	**TOMORROW WILL BE BETTER**	70p*
175239	**A TREE GROWS IN BROOKLYN**	75p*

0427 Wyndham/Circus

	Avery Corman	
004195	**OH, GOD!**	70p* ♦

† For sale in Britain and Ireland only.
* Not for sale in Canada.
♦ Film & T.V. tie-ins.